SIN'S SACRIFICE

A SECOND CHANCE, MC NOVELLA

ELLA KADE

SIN'S SACRIFICE by Ella Kade

ISBN-13: 978-1-950044-67-2 (Ebook Edition)

ISBN-13: 978-1-950044-35-1(Paperback Edition)

Edited by: The Polished Author

Proofreading by: The Polished Author, Amira El Alam

Photographer: Xram Ragde

Cover Model: Anthony

Manufactured in the United States of America.

SIN'S SACRIFICE

Join Ella's mailing list to be the first to know of new releases, free books, sales, and other giveaways!

https://harlowlayne.com/newsletter/

Ten years ago, I left the innocent life I led behind.

One phone call changed everything I thought I knew or wanted.

Now Charlie was back in my life more beautiful than ever, and stirring up feelings I thought were long dead.

How she got mixed up in a life I never wanted for her I'll never know, but with each passing day I spend protecting her now I war with myself on whether or not I should do the right thing and send her packing or if I let my selfish needs take over.

ONE
SIN

THE SOUND of my phone ringing woke me from my pleasant sleep. I slid out from underneath the arm of whichever club slut was in my bed and reached for my phone.

"This better be fucking good," I grumbled, my voice heavy with sleep.

A long silence made me wonder if one of my brothers was fucking with me. They should know better than to make their VP over some stupid shit. Maybe they got one of the prospects to prank me. Whoever it was, was going to be in a world of hurt.

Now that I was awake and pissed, I jumped out of bed, ready to head to the clubhouse to see who wanted to die. "I'm going to kick your mother-fucking ass when I get there."

"Sin?" a sweet voice called my name. Far back in the recesses of my mind, I knew that voice.

"That's me. Who's this?" I gritted out.

"Oh… um, this is Charlotte," she said so quietly I could barely hear her.

"Charlie? Is that you?"

"Yeah," she sniffed.

I was instantly on alert. I hadn't heard from Charlotte since I broke things off with her right after we graduated high school almost ten years ago.

"Is everything okay?" I stood looking out the window only to see the midnight sky and the outline of trees that surrounded our ranch.

"I know you don't want to hear from me, but I didn't know who else to call. I need help."

"Where are you at?" I picked up my jeans from the floor and slipped them on as I asked the question.

"I don't know, but I can drop you a pin." She sniffed again, and I swore I was going to dismember whoever hurt her. Charlotte was too sweet for anyone to ever do her harm. That's why I got rid of her when I did. "Can you please hurry? If he finds me, he'll kill me."

"I'm on my way." The second I disconnected, I pulled my t-shirt over my head and slipped my cut on.

Her text with the address came right as I sat on my bike. I revved the engine and took off. Why the fuck was Charlie in enemy territory on the outskirts of town? It didn't matter. I was going to get her out of the mess she was in, and then maybe I'd see her in another ten years, hopefully, under better circumstances.

Knowing she was in the Satan's Savages' domain, I should have called in a few of my brothers. It could get bad quick if they found me riding down their streets.

Pulling up to the run-down house, I wondered what the hell Charlotte was doing here. She didn't belong in a drug house or even on this side of town. Hell, I was surprised she was still in Diamond after all these years. How I hadn't seen her in all these years was a mystery.

Pulling out my gun, I slowly made my way up to the house. All was quiet, which wasn't a good sign.

What if this was a trap?

Pulling my phone out of my pocket, I dialed the number that called me less than twenty minutes ago. The second the line clicked on, I wasted no time. "Where are you?"

"In the back bedroom," she whispered.

"Is there anyone in the house that you know of?" I tried to peek inside, keeping my back against the house, but the windows were painted over.

"I think so. Up until about five minutes ago, there was a lot of yelling and fighting. Then it stopped all of a sudden."

"Is there a door in the back?"

"I… I don't know. I've never been here before. Are you close?"

"Yeah, Charlie." I turned the corner into the backyard with my gun raised. "Tell me you're not doing this to fuck me over?"

There was a slight gasp on the other end of the line, and then her voice hardened as much as Charlie's voice could. She always sounded sweet, even when she was pissed off. "I wouldn't do that to you."

"I had to ask when you're calling me into enemy territory after not talking to me for ten years."

"And whose fault is that? I'm not the one who ended things out of nowhere."

"That shit doesn't matter right now. I'm coming in the back door, and then we need to get the hell out of here before the Savages know I'm here."

I didn't wait for her to respond before kicking the back door open and stepping inside. The place smelled rank, like piss and stale cigarettes.

The sound of movement behind a closed door caught my attention. Slowly, I moved down the hall, waiting for someone to jump out at any moment. Trying the door handle, I found it locked, which I had expected.

"Charlotte, are you in there?"

"Yeah," came her tepid voice from the other side of the door.

"Stand back. I'm going to kick in the door."

The first thing I saw was Charlotte's long brown mane. It was a tangled mess. Her face was white as snow, with except for a bruise forming on the corner of her mouth and a split lip. She ran toward me like I was her knight in shining armor and threw herself into my chest. The moment her face made contact, she started to sob.

Wrapping my free arm around her, I patted her back. "You're safe now. Don't worry." Guiding her out of the house, I looked around the corner to find three men with bullet holes in their foreheads. Pushing her toward the back door, I kept a lookout for anyone trying to ambush us as I got Charlotte out of there. "Let's go."

Charlotte tried to look back in the direction where the bodies were laid out, but I stepped in front of her and blocked her. "We need to get out of here. Now."

She nodded her head as her body started to tremble. I didn't have time to console Charlie. With my hand at the small of her back, I guided her out of the house and out to the street, where my bike sat at the curb.

Grabbing my helmet, I placed it on her head. It was a little big on her, but it was better than nothing. I was so focused on helping Charlotte get on my bike that I didn't notice the figure who came out of the darkness until it was almost too late. If it weren't for Charlotte's gasp, I might never have known.

Whirling around, someone was moving quickly

across the yard in our direction. He raised his hand and, in an instant, I shot him dead center in the chest.

Charlotte let out a muffled scream, but I paid her no mind. I wanted to get out of here before the cops or the Savages showed up.

Throwing my leg over my bike, I had her started and halfway down the street before I felt Charlotte's small hands clasp in front of my stomach. She rested her helmet on my back, and it almost felt like old times.

Except now, I wasn't the innocent boy she used to know. Now I was the killer, and she saw it firsthand.

I took the road slower with Charlie on my bike, but still fast enough to let the feel of the wind calm the beast that had bubbled to the surface the moment I heard the fear in her voice.

It didn't take long to get back to the compound. I parked in front of my cabin and got off my bike. Now that she was safe, it was time to find out what had happened to cause my high school sweetheart to call me in the middle of the night.

Crossing my arms over my chest, I tried not to be affected by seeing her on my bike and to keep the unwelcome memories at bay. "What happened back there?"

Even from a few feet away, I could see her body start to shake again. "My boyfriend," she swallowed harshly. "Ex-boyfriend got in trouble with some guy named

Roach," she sneered his name. "And to get out of it, he gave me to this Roach guy." Her voice quivered as she wrapped her arms around her middle. "Like I'm some piece of property."

Roach was the president of Satan's Savages. He had no qualms about treating women like property or selling them.

"What else happened?" It made no sense he left her there after acquiring her.

This time when she looked up at me, her eyes were glassy as her chin trembled. "I fought with Terry, my ex. Yelling at him about what he'd gotten himself involved in and how he thought he could give me as payment. The Roach guy slapped me across the face, dragged me into the bedroom, and locked me in. He said if I didn't shut up, he was going to kill me." She looked up at me from under her long lashes. "I think he meant it."

"He did. Roach will kill anyone in his path, and now that he owns you, he's going to want to try the merchandise before he decides to either keep you until you're nothing more than a used-up druggie whore, or sell you to the highest bidder."

Stepping off my bike, she squared her shoulders and lifted her chin. "I'd rather die than let him ever touch me again."

"I won't let him near you ever again." My mind spun on how I could keep Charlotte safe. What kind of loser had she been dating that he'd give her up for his debts? "Come on, let's get some rest, and I'll figure out a plan in the morning with my brothers."

The second we stepped inside, Charlotte stopped dead in her tracks. The club slut from earlier was still in my bed face down with her ass bared to us.

Turning around, she eyed the door like it was the most interesting thing she'd ever seen. "Maybe there's someplace else I can sleep."

There was no way I was letting her stay up at the clubhouse with the rest of the guys. Only the club's senior members had their own cabins on the ranch. The rest stayed in the main building, and I didn't trust one of them not to wander into her room. At least until I warned everyone that she was off-limits.

Grabbing Tanya's clothes off the floor, I shook her awake with one meaty palm. She turned over, displaying her fake-ass tits, and smiled up at me. "Time to go."

"What the hell, Sin?" she cried out as I grabbed her by the arm and hoisted her out of my bed.

"Like I said, it's time to go. You know I don't like to repeat myself. Now go make yourself scarce."

Tanya looked Charlotte up and down and sneered. "You're choosing her over me?"

"Get the hell out!" I shouted and slammed my fist into the wall.

Tanya stepped outside with her clothes held loosely.

"He won't keep you for long. He never does, and once you're out, I'll be back in his bed. You just wait and see."

I slammed the door closed and turned back to find Charlie looking over my place. She ran her hand over the spines of a few books that sat on the wall of bookshelves. "You sure keep interesting company nowadays."

I didn't have to explain myself to her. We'd been over longer than we were together.

"If you want to get cleaned up, there's a bathroom. I'll get you something to wear." I stalked over to my dresser, pulled out a Diamond Kings t-shirt, and threw it at her.

Once Charlie was out of sight, I laid down and stared up at the ceiling, wondering how my life had come back full circle. What was I going to do with her once the sun came up?

The door opened, and out walked Charlotte with my t-shirt on that hung down to her mid-thigh. She looked so right with my clothes on, but I had to remember why I gave her up in the first place.

Charlotte Hunter didn't belong in my world.

TWO

CHARLOTTE

I THOUGHT I'd never fall asleep after the horrific events that happened yesterday. Even after seeing that woman in his bed, it took almost no time at all before I was wrapped in Sin's scent of cloves and sandalwood.

When I wake up, there's an unfamiliar yet inviting warmth on my back and an arm thrown over my waist, pinning me down.

Sin.

"Go back to sleep," his deep morning voice rumbles. It was a voice I longed to hear ten years ago but never had the chance since we were still in high school. Thanks to my overprotective parents, we never got to spend a single night together. They would call or drop by anywhere I claimed to be spending the night. If they only knew they didn't protect their daughter's virtue. Instead of losing my virginity in a bed, I lost it in the backseat of my car, but it was just as special. Back then, it didn't matter the location as long as it was with Sin Matthews. I got my wish with the person I thought I would spend the rest of my life with, only for him to break up with me just as I thought our life together was about to begin.

"I can't. I need to pee, and your arm is making it worse," I grumbled as my bladder protested.

He rolled over to his other side without a word, freeing me. Immediately, I felt the loss and wished I hadn't said anything. Slipping out of bed, I pulled his t-shirt down my legs and rushed into the bathroom to relieve myself.

Wanting to wash last night off of me, I turned the shower water on as hot as it would go and stepped inside. Even though steam was rising steadily in the small room, I couldn't feel the heat. All I could feel was Terry's clammy hand as he offered me up on a silver platter and begged Roach to take me.

How had I not seen the signs that he was in trouble or that he was doing drugs? Was I that desperate for any man's attention I ignored all the signs?

Tears slipped down my cheeks, and soon I was sobbing. I had no idea what to do. I'd been given away like a piece of clothing instead of a human being. Would this Roach guy look for me now that I was gone?

Strong arms wrapped around me and picked me up. When had I sat down and curled in on myself? I tried to push away, but it was no use. Sin was too strong, and no matter how much my brain said it didn't want to be in his arms, my heart was melting and trying to meld itself to Sin.

Sin sat down on the edge of his bed with me in his lap, running his fingers through the strands of my wet hair and murmuring nonsensical things into the crown of my head.

Pressing my head to his chest, he spoke softly, as if he were talking to a caged animal. "Charlie, I promise you're safe here. No one can touch you while you're under my protection."

My heart skipped a beat and broke at the same time hearing him call me Charlie. Sin was the only person to ever call me by that name. Everyone else I knew either called me Charlotte or Lotti. It had been so long since I heard him call me Charlie.

Pushing away, I stood, and only then did I realize I was standing naked in front of him. Diving for the bed, I snatched up the sheet and wrapped it around myself.

A glint of mischief sparked in his chocolate-colored eyes as his lips turned upward. "It's nothing I haven't seen before. When did you get all shy on me?"

Pulling the sheet even tighter to my body, I glared at him. "Around the time you dumped my ass."

Sin jumped to his feet and stormed toward me. "Listen, we both know it was for your own good. What good would have come if we'd stayed together? You didn't approve of the life I wanted to live. We would have ended up fighting all the damn time until we hated each other and then broke up. I saved us the heartache."

"Heartache?" I scoffed. "Don't presume to know how I felt. You broke my heart, Sin. For years, I couldn't let another man into my bed, let alone my heart." He growled and stalked around the room like a caged lion. "You have no right to be upset about me being with other people. You left me, and it's not like you've been living the life of a saint. Last night was proof of that." I pointed to the bed where the memory of the woman still sat.

He stopped dead in his tracks, and when he finally turned to look at me, his jaw was hard as stone. "I never said I was celibate. I haven't been sitting around waiting for your call. It doesn't matter, though. This isn't some fairytale where we're getting back together. Now get dressed so we can head up to the clubhouse. I need to meet with my brothers and form a plan to get you out of this mess."

My fingers dug into the fabric of the sheet. "Oh, the solution isn't killing him? I thought that's what you did."

"Is that what you want? For me to kill the big bad wolf for you so you can go on with your life hating me?"

"I've never hated you, Sin." Okay, that was a lie. I had hated him after he ended this so abruptly, but soon after, I was broken and lost, unable to understand how the man I loved didn't love me back.

"You didn't have to," he muttered. Stalking over to the dresser in the room, he pulled out a black t-shirt with the same emblem as the one I had on. Reaching behind his head, he pulled off the shirt he had on by the neck and dropped it on the floor without a care in the world.

That's when I caught sight of the body that had transformed over the last ten years. Sin had always been in shape, but now he was all man with golden skin covering rippling muscles. The sight instantly had my panties drenched. Turning away before I did something stupid, I went back into the bathroom where my clothes from last night sat folded up on the counter. I quickly changed, wishing I had something else to wear—especially a new pair of underwear.

Sin was waiting for me at the door when I stepped out of the bathroom. "Let's go. They're waiting for us."

I followed behind him, almost in a daze. I wasn't sure what I expected when I called him last night, but it certainly wasn't this. We were headed toward a long narrow building that sat about two hundred yards away.

"What is this place?"

"It's our ranch. Up ahead is the clubhouse." He pointed off to the right to a large barn. "There are the stables."

"Do you still ride?"

"When I can." I watched his body grow tenser as we approached what he called the clubhouse.

"Is it safe for me to be here?"

Turning to look at me over his shoulder, his brows pulled together. "There's no safer place for you than here. If I thought you were in any danger here, I would have taken you somewhere else."

Then why was his body so rigid?

With his hand on the doorknob, Sin stopped to turn and look at me. "Stick by my side unless I tell you otherwise. You got it?"

I nodded. My head was like one of those bobbleheads on the dash of a car as we stepped through into the brightly lit room.

Sitting around two circular tables were six large men. The moment they spotted Sin stalking toward them, they stopped what they were doing.

"Who's the chick?" A big, burly guy asked.

Sin didn't answer. He pulled up two chairs to sit in front of them and stood behind one with an expectant look on his face.

Great. He was going to put me on display.

Only once I sat down did he sit in the seat next to me.

"This is Charlotte," he said in a monotone voice. While his tone stated I was nothing special, the rest of the men who sat in front of us didn't have the same reaction. Some of their eyes widened while others' mouths gaped open. One of them whispered *holy shit*.

"Her piece of shit boyfriend—"

"Ex-boyfriend," I interrupted. There was no way I was going to stay with a man who sold me to the leader of a gang to pay off his debts.

"Anyway, her ex gave her to Roach last night to pay off some debt. When I got there, three men were dead in the living room. Roach wasn't there, but I'm sure he was coming back for her, or he would send someone else there to get her. Someone was coming up on us when we were leaving, and I killed him."

"Shit, man, are you stupid?" A man who exuded power closed his eyes and shook his head.

"I wasn't going to leave her there. You know what he'd do to her," Sin gritted out.

"Was it in his territory?" Another asked.

"Yeah, he wouldn't know our history, but he's going to be looking for her. I'm going to keep her at my place until this shit blows over."

"She can stay here at the clubhouse," one laughed.

Sin stood up in a wide stance and crossed his arms over his chest. The tight fit of his jeans over his ass was drool-worthy. "Not going to fucking happen. She's off-limits."

I was surprised when they all laughed as if they weren't surprised by Sin's declaration. I would have protested, but I had no interest in any of these men, even if they were all hot as fuck. I was sure none of them had any problems getting women with the way they looked. Including Sin. Not that I cared.

"We've got to come up with a plan."

"Agreed, but she probably shouldn't be here for this. Why don't you both grab some breakfast, and we'll call church in an hour?" The man rose and stood in front of Sin for a moment until Sin stepped back out of the way. My natural instinct was to shrink back in fear, but I held my ground. I knew Sin wouldn't let any of these men hurt me. Extending a hand, he smiled at me. "I'm Ruin."

The rest of the guys jumped up and stood in a line. It was almost comical to see these big men acting like schoolchildren, so eager to introduce themselves.

Sin stood to the side with a tick fluttering at his jaw. Once I'd met everyone, he held his hand out for me to take. "Let's get some food in you, and I'll see if there are any clothes here for you to wear until I can send someone to collect your things."

We stopped in a kitchen that had one woman cooking at the stove and another at the sink washing dishes. "All of this is really unnecessary, Sin. I'd never seen that man before, so I doubt he has any idea who I am or where I live. I'm sure if I take a couple of days off work and lie low, he'll forget all about me."

Sin stopped putting food onto the plate he held

in his hand. I noticed he'd picked all of the foods I eat and left off the sausage and grits. Did he seriously remember what foods I didn't like after all these years? "Maybe if this was any other man, but not Roach. He doesn't think like the rest of us do. He's ruthless and won't stop until he gets what's his."

"Still, there has to be somewhere else I can stay. I don't want to be an inconvenience." I took the plate as he handed it over to me before he loaded his own full of scrambled eggs and a heaping pile of bacon.

Grabbing my upper arm, Sin pulled me out of the kitchen and through the room where all the men sat and outside before he spoke. "I'm not going to let that man steal you from your life. Let me and my brothers come up with a plan to keep you safe. We won't keep you from your life any longer than necessary."

"I shouldn't have involved you." This wasn't their fight.

"I'm the one person who can help you right now. Do you think your rich daddy has any idea how to deal with human traffickers?" He spat the words rich daddy like they were the foulest words ever spoken.

"And you do?" I shot back. Sin had no idea I hadn't talked to my parents in years after they wouldn't get behind me going to college for an art major instead of becoming a lawyer or a doctor. Having a daughter as an artist, in their eyes, wasn't something you told your friends about in their social circle.

"More than anyone, you know. Just leave the dirty work to us. Now, let's get you back to my cabin. I'll have one of the women in the kitchen get you something else to wear and set it outside my cabin. Don't let anyone in but me. Are we clear?"

"Yes, master," I rolled my eyes.

The corners of his lips twitched. "I like the sound of that."

THE SECOND I walked back into the clubhouse alone, Ruin, our Prez, was on me. "Is she going to be a problem?"

I continued to walk to the tables they'd all been sitting at when I'd brought Charlie in. "Why would she be a problem?" Ruin raised one brow as he stared at me with a knowing look. "I can separate my past from the present, but what I can't do is let her fall into Roach's hands. You know what he'll do her. She's innocent in all this and doesn't deserve to be sold to the highest bidder after Roach has his fun with her."

Sitting down at the table, I hung my head, trying to wrap my head around the last twelve hours and how Charlie was back in my life again.

"Brother," Risk placed a hand on my shoulder and pressed down. "We won't let anything happen to her.

You know that, but you've got to think rationally about what you want to do. Are you ready to start a war with Satan's Savages?"

Over Charlie? Hell, yes, I am. I'd wage war against God and the devil himself to know she was safe from harm.

Sitting down beside me, Ruin tapped his fingers on the tabletop. "And that's what I'm talking about. You can be a part of the planning, but I think it might be best if you stay out of the action."

Jumping out of my seat, I loomed over my Prez, ready to rip his head off. "Not going to happen. She's my responsibility. I brought her here and put our club in danger. There's no way I won't be a part of taking him down."

Ruin's nostrils flared as he glared up at me, not backing down. "Don't let some chic come between you and the club."

I couldn't help it. Even after all these years, Charlie was still embedded deep in every fiber of my being. I hadn't known what was missing until she crashed into me.

Still, it didn't matter if she was the link to my happiness. I couldn't bring her into my dangerous life, only for her to be hurt by my doing.

"I won't." I wasn't sure if I was trying to convince

them or myself. Either way, I wasn't fooling anyone. Not even myself.

"Alright, let's figure out a way to take down Roach and not start a war," Ruin ruled.

"We could make it look like the Savages are going after the Twisted Angels drug business. Get them to work with us and help take the club down," Wrath suggested with a wicked gleam in his eyes.

Crow stretched out his arms across the table as he spoke. "We can't trust the Angels any more than the Savages. They've been working with each other for far too long and have a longstanding relationship. It will be hard to prove the Savages are turning their backs on them."

Tank was shaking his head before he even started to speak. "Please. No one is more loyal than to their club. If it benefits them, they'll stab you right in the eye without a second thought."

He wasn't wrong. A man was only loyal to his club and nothing else.

Rooster, one of the prospects, walked into the kitchen. "Hey, Roost, can you get one of the girls to wrangle up an outfit for Charlie until one of you can get to her place and pack her a bag?"

"Right away," he shuffled out of the kitchen and went back down the hall he'd come from.

"Maybe you should set her up at one of the safe houses," Axel threw out there.

I swung around to look at him. "Not going to happen." If this kept up, I was going to take on all of my brothers.

Axel raised his hands in the air. "Alright, she stays on the compound."

Cowboy leaned forward with his elbows on the table, and his eyes locked on me. "Hawk has wanted the Prez title with the Savages for a long time. We grew up together, so I think I can convince him to a sit-down. He'd know better than anyone how to take down Roach."

"And what happens if he's placating us and goes back to his Prez with the information we're planning to take him out? We're dead before we even start." I didn't care that Cowboy and Hawk grew up together. Hawk bled for his club, and he'd turn on us without blinking an eye.

"No," Cowboy denied. "Hawk will be down."

"I don't see any other way, brother," Ruin objected. "We don't know how their operations work. We need his intel."

"Fine," I gritted out. "We do this in neutral territory, and I want to be there."

Cowboy looked at Ruin and waited for his head to

nod. Only once he got it did he agree. "I wouldn't have it any other way."

"Good. Set it up. I'm going back to my place."

"Be safe, bro," Ruin called as I stepped out into the sunlight.

I took my time as I walked back to my cabin, trying to imagine it through Charlie's eyes. The ranch was big but not nearly as big as some of the ranches in the area. It was our only legal business, and it barely made us any money. My place wasn't big or beautiful. We built them with our own hands, and it was only big enough for one man and an occasional visitor.

Pulling out my keys, I knocked on the door before opening it. I found Charlie sitting on my bed with her back against the wall, and her knees pulled up to her chest. Her eyes were glassy, and her cheeks were tear-stained.

I strode to the bed and looked her over. She'd changed into a pair of tight jeans and a black tank top. "Did something happen while I was gone?"

She shook her head and sniffed.

"How did I get here, Sin? How did I not see what a bad guy Terry was?"

"Some people are good at hiding who they are. Don't blame yourself. If he didn't want you to see, you wouldn't be able to." I sat down on the edge of the bed. "Are you up for getting a few of your things?"

The bed shook as she moved up to my side and sat beside me. Her hands were clasped in her lap, and her head hung. A curtain of hair hid her face. "I don't think I can ride on the back of your motorcycle right now."

While I didn't enjoy being trapped in a cage, I would concede for her. Just this once. "We can take one of the trucks. Let me grab a set of keys, and we'll be on your way."

"Thank you for helping, Sin. I should have said it last night, but I think I was in shock."

Placing my hand on her knee, I rubbed my thumb over her jean-clad leg. "You don't need to thank me." While I'd blindsided her with our breakup all those years ago, I would do right by Charlie now.

"Yes, I do. You could have left me there, and if you did, who knows where I'd be now?"

I was glad she was finally starting to see reason. If I hadn't answered the phone or decided not to show up, she'd either be on her back while being raped or drugged up in a cell waiting for auction.

"Get your shoes on, and let's get this over with." The sooner I was back here, the happier I'd be. Charlie nodded and slipped off the bed to put her shoes on. "I'll meet you out front."

We had a few trucks we used for transport. None of us liked driving them if we didn't have to. We all liked to feel the wind on our faces and hear the roar of our bikes.

I waited out by an old SUV that we rarely used. If anyone from Satan's Savages saw it outside Charlotte's place, they wouldn't associate it with us. Opening the passenger door for Charlie, I waited until we were both inside before I asked, "Where are you living these days?"

She looked out the passenger window as she spoke. "In the loft building on the corner of Commercial and State."

In one of the nicest parts of Diamond, so nothing had changed. Not even her taste in shitty men.

"What do you do for work?"

"I run the gallery downtown." For a brief moment, she looked at me and then back out again.

"You always did love art. I'm glad you followed your dream instead of doing what your parents wanted."

"Yeah, well… they aren't." Her voice became harder and harder with each word she spoke next. "They cut me off when I wouldn't declare either medical or law as my major."

"Damn, Charlie, I'm sorry to hear that, but it sounds like you're doing alright for yourself. When was the last time you spoke to them?"

She let out a sigh that let me know she didn't want to talk to me about them or anything else. "My sophomore year in college. They thought I'd change my mind after a year, and when I didn't, well," she shrugged. "I had to scramble to get a scholarship and find a cheap place to live."

I stopped myself from reaching over to comfort her. I couldn't be falling back into old habits. Charlie would be out of my life soon enough. "I'm sorry to hear that, but I bet it feels hella good to know you did it all on your own without their help."

This time, she turned back to me and held my gaze. "You know, I've never thought about it like that, but you're right. I'm sure they'd lord it over me if they paid for my college all four years, only for me to decide I didn't want to follow in their footsteps."

"How did you end up with that loser?"

"Which loser?" She laughed bitterly. "There's been a string of them." Charlie bit her lower lip, pulling it between her teeth. Fuck, even after all these years, I still got hard from the simple action. "It doesn't matter their social status, rich or poor. They've all done me wrong. Terry was the last of a long line of men who were wrong for me."

"Was I the first?"

"That remains to be seen. Before last night, I would have said yes, but only because you broke my heart. Now, I'm not so sure." Her eyes brightened as she looked at me the same way she did back when we were in high school. Back when I was in her world.

"I'm still a bad man, Charlie. I'm wrong for you in

more ways than one. Don't delude yourself just because I got you out of a bad situation."

"Don't do that. You didn't say it, but I know you're putting yourself in danger. Not just anyone would do that. It means a lot." Reaching across the console, she put her warm hand on my forearm.

"I am a bad man, Charlie." I shrugged off her hang. "I'm not the same guy you knew in high school, but I draw the line at selling people. I believe each person is their own. The only person you own is yourself."

"And you think I'm the same as I was in high school?" Placing her back to the seat, she narrowed her vivid green eyes at me. "I'm not the innocent girl I once was."

"That may be so, but you're still innocent to my way of life. I'll get you out as soon as you're safe. Not a moment before," I promised. The quicker Charlie was out of my life, the better. I couldn't let my heart open up to her again.

Only I had a feeling it was too late.

FOUR

CHARLOTTE

WHILE I DIDN'T KNOW why Sin broke up with me all those years ago, I knew he wasn't as bad of a person as he thought he was. He may be in a biker gang, but he still had a good heart.

Opening my front door, I watched as Sin took in my place. After seeing the way he lived, I knew he'd go back to thinking he wasn't good enough for me like he did back in high school. Back then, he always hated that he couldn't buy me gifts and didn't have the money to take me to a hotel for our first time. Sin's pride wouldn't let him accept my cash or believe that I didn't care where the first time we had sex happened as long as it was with him.

Sin did everything in his power to make our first time special, and I knew that guy was still there. He was just buried deep down inside.

Even though Sin had only grown hotter over the years, I didn't want him. Well, I did. I wouldn't mind one more roll in the hay with him, but I didn't want to start up what we had before.

"We shouldn't be here long in case they're casing out the joint. Be quick."

He didn't have to tell me twice.

Grabbing a suitcase out of my closet, I threw whatever I saw into it and headed to the bathroom. In less than five minutes, I was in and out, scared anyone might show up to kill Sin and steal me away.

Sin stood sentry in my living room, looking out the windows at the city. "This is a nice place you have here. I'll get you back to your life, and you can forget all of this happened."

Dropping my bag, I doubled over laughing. Wiping my eyes, I stood. How could he really think that? "Do you really believe I'll be able to forget this?"

"With time, I think you will be. You'll find yourself a good guy that will treat you like the queen you are, and you won't remember all the losers that came before him." Even as he said the words, his body stiffened, and his jaw turned to stone.

"You don't know me at all."

"No, I don't. It's been ten years, and we're not the same people we once were. But that doesn't matter.

You'll be back here in your fancy-ass apartment with your nice cushy job before you know it."

There was no sense in arguing with him. Sin was a stubborn bastard, and once he made up his mind, it was next to impossible to change it. If I couldn't convince him he was a good person in the four years we were together, two weeks wasn't enough.

"Maybe I should just get a hotel room until this clears up. That way, I won't cramp your style."

"I can't protect you at a hotel. Our compound is heavily guarded. No one can come in without us knowing about it. If you're uncomfortable with me, I can sleep at the clubhouse."

Taking my suitcase from me, Sin waited while I locked my door. "I'm not going to kick you out of your own place. I can stay at—"

"No way in hell are you sleeping at the clubhouse," he barked out and stomped down the hall. "Not without me there."

"Why? You already declared me off-limits," I followed after him. I wasn't sure why he made the proclamation if he wanted nothing to do with me.

"The things that happen at the clubhouse aren't… you just don't need to see what goes on."

"Are you afraid I'll see something that upsets my delicate sensibilities?" I laughed. When Sin didn't respond to my joke, I found him staring off down the road with the corners of his mouth turned down, and the space between his eyebrows was knitted tight. "What's wrong?"

"Let's get to the truck." With his hand on the small of my back, he pushed me in the direction of the SUV.

"What's going on?" I looked over my shoulder, trying to see what had him in such a rush, but Sin stepped in the way and walked faster.

The locks chirped as Sin rounded the SUV. "Get inside, Charlie."

A sense of dread washed over me as I opened the door and jumped inside at the same moment he threw my suitcase in the backseat. My hands shook as I clicked my seatbelt into place.

The tires screeched as Sin took off down the road. "Sin, talk to me and tell me what's going on."

His fingers around the steering wheel tightened until his knuckles turned white. "There were two guys on motorcycles down the street. It's possible they're Savages."

Turning around, I looked out the back window. "Are they following us?"

"It's too soon to tell." He eyed the rear-view mirror before he looked back out the windshield. "They could be giving us space so they can ambush along the way. Keep your eyes peeled open."

I nodded shakily.

How had this become my life?

"You're going to be fine, Charlie. I promise I won't let anything happen to you, and when I make a promise, I keep it." We went faster down the road, flying past cars and people on the sidewalk.

I wanted to shout at him and say he'd already broken one promise to me, but now wasn't the time to air my grievances with him.

Pulling out his phone, he handed it to me.

I stared down at the lock screen on his phone. It was of a never-ending road and a beautiful sunset on the horizon. "What am I supposed to do with this?"

"Call Ruin and put it on speakerphone." His eyes darted back and forth from the mirrors to out in front of us.

"It's locked."

"Ten, thirty," he muttered with his jaw tight.

My birthday.

I didn't dwell on it, at least not right then, but what did it say that Sin used my birthday as the code to get into his phone?

"What's up, brother?" Ruin answered the phone.

"There were two Savages down the street from Charlie's place. They pulled down a side street, but…"

"You think they'll come out in front of you. We're on it, brother. Where are you at now?"

Sin flicked his gaze toward me. "Only about five minutes from the turnoff."

"We're headed that way. If they try anything, we'll intercept them. Cowboy made the call, and you're meeting tomorrow. We'll get this sorted out soon."

"Thanks, brother."

The phone disconnected without either of them saying goodbye. Men.

"Don't be scared." Sin patted my thigh. "There's a gun in the glovebox if that makes you feel any better."

"How did you know?"

"You have the same tells as you did ten years ago?" He eyed me, picking at the skin around my fingernails.

I stopped instantly and put my hands underneath my legs, so I wouldn't wreck my manicure too terribly.

The sound of motorcycle engines put me on alert. I wasn't sure if it was the good or bad guys.

"It's only my brothers," he reassured me. "With them escorting us back, no one will mess with us."

"I hate that I'm putting you all in this position." I bit my lip.

"Darlin', this is our everyday life. You don't need to worry about us. Just let us keep you safe until Roach is out of the picture."

Did he mean what I thought he meant?

"Don't look so scandalized," he chuckled lightly. "He's a bad man who will get what's coming to him. It would have happened sooner or later. You're just the push we needed."

The truck stopped, and I noticed the gate that led to the property. I hadn't noticed it last night or earlier when we left. Instead of the normal fences most ranches had, the Diamond Kings' was an eight-foot wall of stone. At least at the front.

"Does this wall extend around the whole property?"

"Just the front bit, but don't worry. The rest is still safe. We have motion sensor cameras throughout the rest. No one is getting on our land without us knowing." Pulling in front of his cabin, he turned to me. "What do you say we take a ride and I show you?"

Even though I wanted to say no, the pride in his voice had me saying the opposite. I didn't want to disappoint Sin.

A crooked smile spread across his face. "I'll have one of the prospects get the horses ready while you get changed."

I followed him inside and watched as he laid my suitcase on the bed. "Make yourself comfortable. You don't have to live out of your suitcase while you're here."

"Thanks," I muttered as I unzipped my suitcase and looked through it for anything that resembled horseback riding wear. If I had known there would be an opportunity, I might have brought different clothes.

Instead, I picked a pair of dark-washed jeans, the pair of low-heeled boots I had on since last night, and the t-shirt Sin gave me to sleep in last night. Pressing it to my nose, I caught the light smell of clove and sandalwood. Just smelling it caused my muscles to relax while, at the same time, arousal to shoot through me just like it did back in high school.

I could hear noises outside, letting me know Sin was waiting for me. I changed quickly and was shocked to see two horses outside the cabin. It had been a long time since I'd last been on the back of a horse.

"It's like riding a bike," Sin murmured as he brushed by me.

"Can you help me up?"

Without a word, Sin was behind me with his hands on my waist, hoisting me up. "This here is Trixie. She's a gentle soul. You can sit back and relax." He ran his hand up her neck and caressed her face. Sin had always loved horses. They brought a sense of peace to him that nothing else ever could.

"And who do you have?" His horse was tall and black, which I was sure was the reason he chose him to begin with.

"Brimstone." He flashed me a smile.

"He's beautiful."

"Yeah, he is." With one foot in the stirrup, he swung

his other leg over Brimstone. "I'll keep a slow pace. At least until you're comfortable."

Sin was true to his word. We went slow as he pointed out other members' cabins and where cameras were set up. He was right. His life was dangerous. Why else would they have the security they did? A little over an hour later, we came to a stop at a creek running through the property.

"Are you hungry?"

"Yeah, we should probably head back." I pulled on my reins to turn back the way we came when Sin dismounted.

"I thought we could eat here. It's a nice day out with a breeze to keep us cool. What do you say?" Even as he asked, he pulled a blanket out of his saddlebag and laid it out on the ground. Next, he pulled out a big brown bag.

"You packed us a lunch?" How long had it taken me to get dressed?

"It's not much. Just a couple of sandwiches, some potato salad, and fruit."

Still, it was more than anyone had done for me in a long time.

With a hand extended, he stood at my side. "Do you need help down?"

"Thanks," I answered as I let him help me down. I sat and watched as he folded himself down onto the blanket and pulled out our food. "I never thought of you as the picnic type of guy."

"Yeah, me either. Don't read too much into it. It's only a blanket on the ground and a sandwich."

Then why did he pick by the water under a tree?

He handed over a sandwich and then set out two small containers of potato salad. "I hope you still like turkey, Colby Jack, and mayonnaise."

"Are you still putting mayo on yours even though you don't like it?" He would make us a sandwich back in the day to share, and with every bite, he would grimace. It didn't take me long to realize that Sin hated the taste of mayonnaise. Still, he kept making us sandwiches with it because I liked it.

He flashed me a grin as he shook his head. "Nah, I gave that up."

Just like he gave me up.

"It's beautiful out here. I'm glad you have all this."

"It is. I never thought I'd have anything of worth to my name." He took a bite of his sandwich, taking a quarter of it with him. It looked like he still ate like it might be his last meal.

We ate in silence. I took in the blowing leaves and the horses drinking at the water. I spotted a cabin in the distance.

"Whose place is that?"

"No one's right now. I guess whoever gets an old

lady will take it." The way he said it made it seem like that wasn't a possibility.

"And what's an old lady?"

"It's what we call our women. The ones who are committed to us and us to them."

"And what, none of you are into monogamy, so the house goes untouched?"

Sin chewed the rest of his sandwich and washed it down with a long swallow from his beer bottle. "The women we want by our side for the long term aren't meant for the life we live."

Then maybe you should think about a different life.

"Sounds like a lonely life."

"I got my brothers, and that's all I need."

I wasn't sure if he was trying to convince himself or me.

Wanting to change the subject and thoughts of Sin with dozens, if not hundreds of women, I shifted to look out at the water. "I'm going to need to go back to work tomorrow."

"Not going to happen. You'll need to call in sick or take a vacation or something."

My blood was boiling by the time I turned to look at him. "You don't get to dictate my life. Not anymore."

"You better believe it. I'm protecting your ass, and I can't do that while you're sitting in some art gallery with your fancy-ass customers."

The way he talked about my work, it was like he had something against it that I didn't understand.

Gritting my teeth, I stood, ready to go back to my cell because that's what this suddenly felt like. I was locked down against my will, and I had zero say in what was done. "I can only take a couple of days off before a big shipment comes in that I need to be there for. If I don't show up, I'll lose my job."

Sin huffed and balled up the trash before shoving it back into the bag. "One thing at a time. Tomorrow I have a meeting, and after that, I'll figure out a way for you to be at your job. You won't be alone, though. Make no mistake about that."

After that, he didn't speak as he helped me back onto my horse, and we headed back to the cabin.

I knew I shouldn't be angry with him, but I couldn't help it. Sin didn't even discuss anything with me. He just bossed me around and expected me to dutifully do as he said. He would soon learn I wasn't the same girl he knew back in high school. I wouldn't let him ruin my career. I'd lost too much to follow my dream.

COWBOY BLOCKED the entry into the bar we were meeting at. "You need to calm down, brother. Hawk isn't going to fuck us over. Even if he doesn't like what we have to say, he won't narc us out."

"I'm sorry if I don't trust him as much as you do. I get that you grew up with him, but he's been with his club—"

"I hear you," Cowboy gritted out. "For me, try to give him the benefit of the doubt."

Giving him a nod, I followed him inside a neutral bar that neither club did business in. I scanned the few people who sat scattered throughout the establishment. None of them looked like any of the men I knew as Satan's Savages.

Hawk sat in a booth in the very back, his arms spread out along the top without a care in the world. He jumped up the second he saw Cowboy. "What's up?" They gave each other a manly bro hug thing. I only tipped my chin in his direction.

We sat on the other side of the booth, and I stared at the man called Hawk. He had brown hair cut short, brown beady eyes, and a long nose. I let them shoot the shit for a couple of minutes before I couldn't take it any longer and had to step in.

"Did Cowboy tell you why we're here?" I interrupted.

"Only that you guys had a problem and that I might be able to help. What's going on?"

"Someone from my VPs past was given to your Prez, and to say Sin is unhappy is an understatement," Cowboy started.

"Ah," Hawk nodded his head. His little beady eyes focused on me. "Yes, he's definitely noticed something was missing. She must be something special. He got called away on an emergency and immediately sent someone to collect her. With his property gone and a dead prospect left on the lawn, *my* Prez is one unhappy man."

I wanted to ask him how he thought selling a woman was okay, but I kept my mouth closed. If I offended him, he'd be less likely to help us out.

Leaning forward, I clasped my hands out in front of

me. "The only way we see this panning out for the good of everyone is to make him a dead man."

Those cold brown eyes of his drilled into me. "He won't give up until he's six feet under. I don't see how I come into play here."

"We need help, brother. I know you don't approve of all the shit he's led to your club, and you've wanted a seat at the head of the table for far too long. You help us take him out, and you'll get what you want."

Hawk was already shaking his head. "I can't help you kill him. If anyone found out…"

"We're not asking you to kill him for us. Only to give us information on where he might be and the best time to take him out."

"Only," Hawk laughed. "All of this over some bitch."

"Not just some bitch." Standing, I leaned over the table until I was in his face. "She's mine, and no one touches her."

Hawk leaned back and laughed. "Damn, who knew a gash could get you so up in arms? He's a paranoid son of a bitch. We never know where he'll sleep from one night to the next. Good thing for you, he likes to be alone with whatever new plaything he has for a couple of days after getting them. With your girlie missing, he's got a whole shipment of women he wants to *try* out."

Why did he have such a hard-on for Charlie?

"Is he normally this… possessive over a woman he just… acquired?" Cowboy asked delicately.

Hawk took a long sip of his beer before he spoke. "No, he likes to have his fun and then get rid of them. Does he know her connection to you?"

Shaking my head, I answered. "I hadn't spoken to her in ten years." And I seriously doubted she was talking about me to anyone.

"Maybe he figured it out." He gave a one-shoulder shrug. "I can't say. All I know is he wants her back something fierce." Hawk stood and slapped his hand down on the table. "When I know something useful, I'll get in touch. It shouldn't be more than a couple of days."

"Thanks, brother." Cowboy gave him a fist bump.

My head was reeling. We were nowhere closer to taking Roach out than we were before we met. Nothing Hawk said gave me confidence he wouldn't rat us out, either.

"We got nothing from that meet," I growled out before signaling a waitress. "Two shots of tequila and a beer."

"Sure thing, hon," she smiled sweetly at me like I hadn't just grunted out my order to her.

"He can't give us what he doesn't know, and we know Roach is a slippery bastard. When he knows a location where we can get to him, he'll let us know."

"Either way, we need to ramp up security at the ranch. If he knows Charlie's there, he'll come for her."

Cowboy nodded, his brows furrowed. "Your girl is pretty and all, but if her boyfriend gave her to him that night, then why—"

"I'm thinking the same thing. He had to know of her beforehand and wanted her. That's how her junkie boyfriend knew he could pay off his debt with her."

"Makes sense to me. It's not good if he's obsessed with her." Hawk muttered under his breath as the waitress sat down my drinks.

I threw back both the shots in rapid succession and slammed the glasses on the tabletop. "It's not wise for him to try to think he owns what's mine. When I get my hands on him, I'm going to cut off his dick and shove it down his throat before I spill his entrails on the floor."

"And I'll be right by your side. Make no mistake about it. Let's get out of this godforsaken place. This place makes my skin crawl," Cowboy shuttered.

That made me chuckle. Cowboy liked to spend ninety-nine percent of his time outdoors. Hell, he even slept outside under the stars. He was only indoors when he used his room at the clubhouse while with a woman or when we were having church. Any other time, you'd never find him inside. I got it, I really did, but Cowboy was almost allergic to being indoors.

Slapping down some cash on the table, we headed

outside. I scanned the street to make sure Hawk didn't have a crew outside waiting with him.

"I want to get back to Charlie. She's not going to be happy to be away from her life until we hear more about Roach. I've got to come up with a way for her to be able to go to work and have protection."

"Oh," Cowboy laughed. "I'm sure she's going to love that."

He lifted a brow at me as he straddled his bike. "Maybe calm her down in other ways before you give her the news."

That wasn't happening. I knew nothing good would come from me sticking my dick in Charlie.

Cowboy chuckled and shook his head at me. "If you need one of us to take the reins, I'd be more than happy to help you out."

"Not going to fucking happen." I ground my molars until I felt a layer of enamel scrap off. "No one fucking touches her."

He held his hands up. "I was only trying to help out."

I flipped him off before starting my Harley.

The ride back wasn't long enough. I was still pissed off that nothing was working in my favor, and I knew it was only going to get worse once I stepped foot inside my place.

Lighting up, I inhaled a long drag and held it as long as I could in one last attempt to calm down.

My front door swung up with Charlie standing at the entrance with her arms crossed over her chest.

"Can you let me finish this smoke first?"

Charlie stepped out, her bare feet hitting the grass. "I'm not the naïve girl I was back in high school. I can handle whatever you throw at me. I'm not going to let you dictate my life without having any say in it."

"I can accept that, but you need to remember that I know this world, and you have to listen to my expertise on this matter."

She stomped forward, her eyes blazing. "I had no idea what I was getting myself involved in when I met Terry."

"You should have known he was a loser." I hadn't met the guy, but anyone who would sell his woman off to pay a debt deserved to be six feet under.

"Perhaps I should have, but that's on me. Not you. Let me be a part of the planning as much as you can." Her green eyes welled with tears. "Can you do that?"

I nodded and snuffed out my cigarette on the bottom of my boot. "As much as I can. If I say you can't be a part of something or can't know something, it's for your well-being. There are some things you should never know."

There was a lot she shouldn't know about our club. A lot, especially since this was a temporary arrangement.

"I can live with that." She gnawed on her bottom lip before she spoke. "How was your meeting?"

"Uneventful. The only thing we know is their Prez is actively looking for you. It seems you caught his interest."

"What? How?" she shrieked and took an unsteady step back. "I never even met him before I was hauled in front of him."

Pushing off my bike, I grabbed her around the waist and hauled her back into my cabin. "My guess is your man mentioned you one too many times and got Roach interested. He probably saw you out on the street or got curious about you and sought you out. However it went down, he was interested and wanted to sample the goods before he decided what he wanted to do with you."

"No," she whimpered and rested her forehead on my chest.

Wrapping her in my arms, I rested my chin on the crown of her head. "I'm not going to let that happen, so there's no need to worry."

"Simple words aren't going to placate me." Charlie rubbed her forehead against my pec. "I know I shouldn't want him dead, but…"

"If it makes you feel better, he won't stop until he's dead. You won't have to witness a thing."

"Thanks."

"You don't have to keep thanking me. I would do this for anyone who was in his sights."

Charlie pushed off me. "Good to know. Is it going to be safe for me to go to work on Monday?"

"I haven't figured out the logistics yet. The one thing I can tell you is you won't be going alone."

"Great, I might as well quit now because one look at one of you in your leather cut and tattoos, and I'll be fired."

"Your bosses sure are judgmental fucks if they're going to judge us by the way we look." I ran my hand down my cut and pulled at the edges. "I'll have you know, for the most part, if we want to, we can hide in plain sight."

"Whatever." She rolled her eyes. "I need to get some fresh air. Is it safe for me to go out there on my own?"

Leaning my hip against the kitchen counter, I crossed my ankles. "You're free to go wherever you want on the ranch." I wasn't going to tell her there would always be someone watching her everywhere she went from now on. I had a feeling she wouldn't be too happy about that.

I typed out a quick text to Rooster, telling him to trail Charlie but keep back far enough that she wouldn't see him.

The second she left the cabin, I got to work. I had no idea how long Charlie would be gone, but I knew she wouldn't appreciate what I was about to do.

Going to my safe, I put in the code and opened it up to pull out a few of my small tracers. I placed one in her purse, in the sole of the other pair of shoes she brought, and the last in the collar of her jacket. I couldn't predict what she would wear, but I wanted my bases covered. Once I had the chance, I would put a tracing program on her phone. If anything happened to her, I could only hope she had one of the four on her.

Now I just had to figure out what to do about Charlie going to work. I knew she wouldn't let me protect her all day, so I'd have to find someone else who could blend. I left my place and headed to the clubhouse to speak with my brothers.

Tank, Wrath, and Crow were sitting at the bar with Eagle, our other prospect, behind the bar serving them. Eagle's bald head gleamed under the lights as he extended a bottle of beer to me.

"Where's your better half?" Crow laughed.

Sitting down on the stool next to Wrath, I drank down half of my beer in one go. "Taking a walk to get away from me."

He patted me on the back and shook his head. "Trouble in paradise already, Veep?"

"She'll be gone as soon as I take out Roach. Until then, she is adamant about going to work. That's where I need one of you guys. Who's willing to blend in and stick with her? I think a couple of the guys could be on rotation."

Tank leaned forward until our eyes locked. "Where does she work?"

"At the art gallery downtown."

"Good luck with that," Tank laughed. "Are we supposed to wear suits and shit?"

"Fuck if I know. I've never been to a gallery." With my elbows on the bar, I hung my head and ran my fingers through my hair, pulling at the ends. "I don't know what I'm doing here."

"No shit," they all laughed.

"Don't worry. We'll keep her safe, and soon, you'll be rid of her. Maybe you should stay here tonight and get a little pussy. It might make you relax a little bit."

They were probably right, but I couldn't do it. Not with Charlie so close to me.

Once she was gone, my life could go back to normal.

SIX

CHARLOTTE

I SPENT two hours walking the ranch. It was beautiful, and with each minute that passed, I relaxed a little more. I knew it wasn't Sin's fault I was in this situation. My stupidity put me in this situation.

Wanting a sense of normalcy, I decided to immerse myself in making a home-cooked meal. It was one of the ways I calmed myself when my life felt out of control.

I knew Sin didn't have any food at his place, and he wouldn't let me go to the grocery store, so I headed to the clubhouse. I wasn't sure how welcome I'd be when I stepped inside.

The entire room turned, and all eyes were on me. I knew my smile was timid as I slowly walked toward them.

"Sin is at the stables. If you want, I can have one of

the prospects walk you down there." A man who I thought was named Ruin said.

"Oh, I'm not looking for him. I wasn't sure if I could get someone to take me to the grocery store…" I knew it was a long shot, and going by the hard look set upon each and every one of their faces, I was shit out of luck. "Or maybe someone could go for me."

"The girls keep the kitchen packed. Why don't you have yourself a look in there, and if there's something you need, we can send out for it." Ruin turned back to them as if I wasn't there.

"Okay, thank you. I'm sorry to bother you."

"No bother, darlin'," one of the men said. "Do you know where the kitchen is?"

"Yes." I ducked my head and moved as quickly as possible without looking like I was sprinting away.

They weren't wrong. The kitchen was more like its own grocery store. It probably had to be with as many men who were here on any given day. I wasn't sure if they all lived here or not, but if they did, it would have to cost a fortune to feed them all. I wasn't sure what I wanted to cook, so I looked through the refrigerator, which was filled with more fresh produce than most grocery stores. Not really, but close. It was full of peppers, tomatoes, green beans, apples, oranges, lettuce, carrots, and so much more. Then there was the fresh meat ranging from sausage to chicken thighs. This refrigerator probably rivaled some restaurants. I plucked out a handful of tomatoes, thinking I could make a nice sauce with them. Moving into the pantry, I hoped I'd find the ingredients to make my own pasta. Sure enough, it was filled to the brim with spices and dry goods.

A redhead popped in with a soft smile. She had curves for days that had me envious. "I heard you were in here. I brought you a bag to carry your goods in."

"Oh, thank you. I was sure I'd have to make a few trips, and by then, they," I nodded my head in the direction of the men sitting out in the other room. "Would be tired of me."

"Oh, don't worry about them. They don't even know you're in here."

Great, so I was unmemorable. Sin and his friends sure knew how to make a girl feel like dog poop that they had stepped in.

"Not like that." She laid her delicate hand on my arm. Her touch was warm and comforting. "There are always people coming and going. If you're not deemed a threat, they tend to put you out of their minds while they're working."

I guess that was somewhat better.

"What are you planning to make?"

"Some type of tomato sauce and handmade pasta. I'd love to make some garlic bread to go with it, but…" I looked around and didn't see what I needed to make bread.

"I can go out and get anything else you need. Just say the word. I do all the food shopping here."

"You stock this," I indicated all the food surrounding us.

"Yeah, I know it looks like a lot, but it goes fast. Me and a couple of the other girls, we do the cooking most nights. If the men are all out on a run, we typically head into town and grab a bite to eat." She reached out her hand. "By the way, I'm Layla."

I took her hand in mine. "I'm Charlotte."

"I know who you are. Everyone does. We did before you came."

"What do you mean you all knew who I was before I showed up here?" How was that possible? Was Sin keeping tabs on me?

She lightly laughed like it was obvious why they all knew of me. "Everyone knows about the woman Sin gave up."

Gave up?

Her eyes widened. "Maybe I shouldn't have said anything. I should be going. If you need anything else from the store, let me know. I'll drop the bread by Sin's place when I get back."

"Thanks," I muttered. I wondered how many times she'd been in Sin's cabin. No, I wasn't going to think that way. Sin could do whatever he wanted, whenever he wanted.

Had Sin lied to them in a pity attempt? No, that wasn't him. But why would he say he gave me up? Sin cheated on me. I saw it with my own eyes.

Packing up what I needed, I slipped out of the kitchen as quietly as possible, hoping no one noticed me. What did they know about me? That I was a fool for thinking Sin loved me, and we'd always be together back in high school.

Two hours later, I was cutting the pasta with a pizza cutter. Not ideal, but it was the best option when Sin showed up.

"Holy fucking shit, does it smell good in here." He moved in close to me, taking deep breaths. "What are you making?"

"It's nothing too fancy. Just simple pasta with a tomato sauce," I answered. I didn't want to spend too much time in the kitchen, nor did I want to use up any food they planned to use. I tried to keep it simple.

"You know you don't have to cook. The girls cook up at the clubhouse, and we all go there most nights."

I kept cutting the squares and forming them. It was like a farfalle, but without the edges. "I'm well aware, but I wanted to. It calms me, and I needed it."

"Even after your walk?" He raised a brow. "What's got you so up in arms?"

Stopping, I placed my hands on my hips and turned to him. "Because the fact that I have no say in what's happening in my life isn't enough?"

"I'm only doing this to keep you safe. Being alive right now is more important."

I did like being alive, even if my boyfriend had thrown me away like I meant nothing to him, and I had to spend time with another ex who I never thought I'd see again.

"Can I ask you a question?"

Sin leaned his hip against the counter and crossed his arms over his chest. "You can ask, but it doesn't mean I'll answer. There are some things that aren't safe for you to know."

"I'm not asking for top secret information about your club. I met Layla when I was in the kitchen, and she said something interesting."

"Oh yeah, what's that?" He smirked.

"That they all know of me before I got here, and you gave me up."

The smirk instantly died off his face, and he shifted, looking away from me. Instantly, I knew he was going to lie to me. What I didn't understand was why. "Layla needs to learn to keep her mouth shut. Pay no mind to her. She means well, but she likes to gossip and gets things twisted up."

Now it was my turn to cross my arms over my chest. I moved to stand right in front of him. He needed to see my face as I spoke. "I think she was telling me the truth. I remember getting introduced to all of those men, and it wasn't the first time they'd heard my name."

"I'm sure they've heard it once or twice over the years. It doesn't mean anything. Is there anything you need help with?" It didn't escape my notice he changed the subject, but I wasn't going to push. It made no difference to me. I didn't plan to spend much time around the others, anyway.

"It's almost done, but Layla was supposed to drop by with some bread so I can make garlic bread. Can you check to see if she's back yet?"

"Sure," he drew out the word.

While I waited for the pasta water to be ready, I put together some butter, garlic, and parsley. Sin was back before the water started to boil.

Setting down the bread, he leaned back on the counter. "So, there's a party up at the clubhouse tonight. I thought you might like to relax and maybe have a little fun."

Letting loose would be nice, but I wasn't sure I could

handle seeing a bunch of women fawning over Sin. Or worse, him touching them or all the guys wondering why I was causing problems for them.

"It's just a few people sitting by the fire, drinking, and having fun. If you get overwhelmed, we can come back here."

"I would hate to…" cock block was the word I wanted to use, but I didn't want him to know how I felt. I didn't know why I wasn't still pissed off at him. He'd lied to me less than ten minutes to go, and he broke my heart. I still wasn't over the betrayal, but I knew it was for the best when I looked at the man Sin had become. I was nothing like the women I'd seen around here.

"I won't leave your side. I promise."

That wasn't what I wanted, but once he said the words, it did make me feel better.

"Let's go after dinner, which won't be much longer. I just need to slice the bread, put the butter mixture on it, and put it under the broiler for a few minutes while the pasta cooks."

He watched me as if he'd never seen a person butter bread before. "I thought pasta took at least ten minutes."

"That's only when using store-bought. This is fresh. It only takes a couple of minutes."

"Why didn't you ever cook like this when we were together?" He asked over my shoulder.

"Because I rarely cooked back then. I… started. It

helps center me." I didn't mention how my aunt taught me to cook to get my mind off the man who broke my heart.

"Well, whatever the reason, I appreciate you cooking as long as I get to eat some of this fine-ass food."

Looking over my shoulder, I smiled at him. "Of course, you get to eat it. I didn't make all of this just for me, and it's certainly not enough to feed the army of men outside these walls."

"They are a hungry bunch. Since you've done all the hard work, let me see if I can wrangle up a couple of plates and some silverware for us to use."

"Yes, it is pretty sparse in your kitchen. I'm guessing you never eat in here."

"It's no fun eating by yourself when there are always at least half a dozen men a few hundred feet away." He set two plates down on the kitchen counter along with a fork for each of us.

Removing the pot from the burner, I moved to strain the pasta at the sink. "If you never eat here, why do you have anything to begin with?"

"Yeah, the women deck out the places when someone moves in with things they think we might need. If it wasn't for them, this place would probably only house my clothes and a bed."

That was kind of sad.

Since Sin barely had the essentials, I left the pasta in

the pot and the sauce in the saucepan. I added a piece of garlic bread to each of our plates before we helped ourselves. I couldn't take a bite of my food until I watched Sin's reaction. He didn't disappoint. A low groan filled the small area.

"Damn, this has to be the best damn meal I've ever had." He looked up from his plate and motioned to mine. "Aren't you going to eat?"

I took a bite and let the acid from the tomatoes and the garlic fill my palate. "I wanted to see if you like it first."

"I don't think you ever have to worry about that. If you want to keep making dinners, I'll happily eat them." He shoved a large bite of food in his mouth. He closed his eyes, and a soft look came over his face. It was a look I never thought I'd see grace his face ever again. It used to only be reserved for me. It made me wonder who else got to see that look on his face.

After he'd finished off his plate full of food, he set down his fork and placed his hand on his stomach. "Damn, woman. I think I need a nap after that."

Sin stuffing himself was a wonderful compliment.

"Two of the guys have volunteered to be at the gallery in civilian clothes. All you have to do is tell them what you need or what to do, and they'll be in the shadows in case anything happens."

"Thank you, Sin. I know they won't like it, but it means a lot. They're willing to watch out for me."

I was shocked when Sin stood and took his plate to the sink and then watched as he washed and rinsed his plate. I guess he wasn't a total lost cause after all. "My brothers will do anything to help me and those I care about."

"I guess I should be lucky to be one of those people."

He took my plate from me and washed it as well. Once he was done, he turned around. The softness from earlier was long gone. "What do you say we go party?"

"Lead the way."

SEVEN
SIN

I COULD FEEL Charlie's hesitation as we stepped into the backyard. Maybe it was the orange-red glow that was lighting up the sky. Either that or she was afraid of the guys.

"We can head back anytime you want. Just say the word."

She nodded meekly.

"What do they know about me?" She quietly said as everyone came into view.

I turned to stand in front of her and blocked her view. There was no way I was going to tell her they knew *everything*—more than she even knew. "That your name is Charlie, and you're from my past."

"Your past," she repeated. "Whatever. Just get me a drink, so I can forget about my life for a little while."

Two hours later, I was the one who didn't want to be

here any longer. Charlie was sipping on her fourth drink, and it looked as if she was as much of a lightweight as she was back in high school. She was laughing non-stop with Cowboy and Tank and touching their arms constantly. Luckily, they knew to stay the hell away, even if it didn't seem like it. I was close to punching both of them in the face and threatening to cut their balls off any second.

Charlie leaned into me and rubbed her hand up my arm. "You don't look like you're having any fun," she pouted.

"All that matters is you're having fun and getting along with my brothers."

"They're not as scary as I thought they were. They're actually really nice." She tried to whisper, but everyone in a five-foot vicinity heard her.

"Aw, we like you too, Ms. Art Gallery," Tank chuckled.

"Yeah, we thought you were going to be stuck up, but you're actually pretty cool. Too bad you'll be gone soon," Cowboy added.

Charlie slouched down in her chair; her body deflated. "Yeah."

"You don't want to hang out with us dirty men forever." I patted her silky, soft hair. "You'll go back to your life and forget all about us."

"It's not so bad here. I like that you're all a family. I

can see that here. Even with the slutty women." Charlie wrinkled her nose as one of the club sluts was giving a lap dance. "I miss having a family." She sniffed and then jumped up. "I need to use the bathroom." She hurried off and dashed inside the back of the clubhouse.

Tank looked after Charlie and then at me. "Maybe you should go after her."

"What am I supposed to say? She can come hang out anytime?"

"It's obvious you still love her, and she still loves you. Why not be with her?"

"Are you delusional? She doesn't belong here on our dusty ranch."

"I don't know. She seems like she likes it."

"She's here because I'm trying to keep her out of danger, not immerse her life into our world. It wouldn't be fair to start something knowing it would have to end."

"Just go after her before you regret it."

I flipped them both off.

I bumped into Charlie as I opened the door and stepped inside. "Are you okay?"

"Yeah," her voice cracked. Her head was down.

"Charlie, look at me." When she shook her head, making her hair go flying, I knew she was anything but okay. Placing a finger under her chin, I lifted her head until I saw the tears streaking down her cheeks. A deep pit in my stomach formed as I wiped her tears away with the pads of my thumbs. "Why are you crying?"

"I don't know. My emotions are all over the place." Her lip quivered. "I wanted to hate you, and I do, but then I don't until I see the boy who broke my heart. Then I just hate you more."

"And you should. I hate what I had to do, but then I see what you've become, and I couldn't be prouder, and I knew I did the right thing."

Charlie's brows puckered as she tipped her head up to look at me, her emerald eyes shining. "What are you talking about?"

Yes, why had I opened my big mouth?

The music died, and a hush came over the night. It only lasted a second before my brothers rushed past us and into the clubhouse. Ruin growled out two syllables. "Clubhouse."

"What's going on?" Her voice was high and on alert.

"I have no idea. Can you get yourself back to my cabin?" I was torn between needing to see she was safely inside and finding out what had changed the night from fun to serious in a heartbeat.

She was already nodding her head before I finished speaking. "I'm perfectly fine on my own. Go see what's happening."

"Are you sure you're okay?" I hated to rush off when

she was upset, but maybe it was for the best after I said shit I shouldn't.

"I'm sure," she nodded her head a little too quickly. Turning on her heels, she scampered away. I stood at the mouth of the door until she was lost in the shadows.

Stepping into church, I sat to Prez's right and waited for him to begin. Thirty seconds later, he knocked the gavel on the table and cleared his throat. "We got an alert a few minutes ago that one of Savage's men tried to breach us on the northeast side. They've got to know your girl is here. Tonight, it was one guy, but the next time it will be more."

"We've got to hit him where it hurts," Wrath pounded his fist on the table.

I narrowed my eyes. "And how are we going to do that? We're waiting for Cowboy's man to give us a heads up on where Roach will be."

"If we strike, then he'll come out of hiding, and we can take him out then. Easy."

"As much as I hate to say it, we don't want to start a war with them. If we take out Roach and Hawk takes over, we'll have a truce between the clubs."

Half the guys at the table nodded their heads.

"If Hawk doesn't come up with something in the next few days, then we'll have to strike. We will not let the Savages get the upper hand," Ruin ordered. "I want to double the security on the perimeter and in the surveillance room until this matter is settled."

Banging the gavel again, Ruin stood. "Meeting is adjourned. Now let's get back out there and party."

"I'm going to head back to my place and make sure Charlie's okay," I announced as we walked out.

"Do a shot with your Prez before you head out. You've been sulking all night and need to get your head out of your ass," he laughed. "Does it have anything to do with your girl talking to Tank and Cowboy?"

"Nothing." I threw back the shot of tequila and saluted Ruin. I wasn't going to talk to him or any of them about Charlie when, for some reason, they were trying to get us back together.

Forgetting myself, I didn't knock as I made my way inside my cabin. Charlie was huddled up on the bed like a scared little bird until she saw it was me. Jumping off the bed, she ran and threw herself at me.

"Oh my god, Sin, I was so scared something happened to you, or they were coming for me." She shook in my arms as she tried to catch her breath.

"I'm sorry. I didn't mean to worry you." I smoothed my hand down her silky hair. "There was an attempt to get on the property, but it was handled."

Her head tipped back until our eyes locked. "Does that mean they know I'm here?"

"We had no beef with them before..." I let her fill in

the blank. I didn't want to be the one who told her. Charlie would only feel bad she brought trouble to our doorstep.

"I hate that I'm causing trouble. If it becomes too much…" her lower lip trembled.

"Never going to happen." I threaded my fingers through her hair and forced her to look at me. "What would happen to you if Roach got you now would be a thousand times worse than before. The only way he's getting his hands on you is over my cold, dead body."

"Don't say that." Her hands ran up between my pecs and rested on my shoulders. "I don't want anything to ever happen to you."

"I feel the same way about you, Charlie. You don't need to worry. I've been in bad situations before and got myself out of them. This is no different. And with my brothers by my side, we can't fail."

Charlie surged up on her tippy-toes and crashed her mouth to mine. Shocked, I opened my mouth. Her warm tongue slipped inside and ran along mine. I knew I should have stopped her. Stopped this, but I couldn't. One taste was all I wanted, and after this, I'd keep my distance.

She moaned into my mouth. The sound broke something inside of me. Running my hands down her sides, I gripped her juicy ass and pulled her flush to me, grinding my ever-hardening dick into her.

Fuck.

Nothing had changed. With a single touch from Charlie, my dick would turn to stone.

Picking her up, I moved toward the bed. Her legs wrapped around me as her fingernails scratched at my scalp. With her body pressed to mine, I crawled up the bed and laid her out before me. All rational thought left me when I saw her pretty pink lips swollen from our kiss and the way her chest heaved as she tried to catch her breath. I wasn't sure how it was possible, but she was even more beautiful than she had been. The Charlie before me was all woman, and I wanted to get to know each and every one of her curves.

Dipping down, I lifted the hem of her shirt and ran my tongue around the rim of her belly button. Her skin was the perfect mix of salty and sweet. Charlie arched her back and moaned, her thighs pressing against my sides, holding me in place. Pushing her shirt up higher, I kissed and licked each new inch of skin that was unveiled.

Getting up on my knees, I pulled her shirt the rest of the way overhead. My heart might have stopped at the sheer lace bra she wore. Her pink nipples puckered and begged for my mouth.

"Fuck, you're even more beautiful," I murmured before taking one stiff peak into my mouth and swirling my tongue around the lace that covered it. My other hand plucked and twisted at her other nipple. She ground her core into my leg as little gasps left her lips.

"Fuck me, Sin. I want you," she moaned as she rode my leg harder. "Fill me up with your big cock."

Even though I knew it was wrong, I couldn't deny her. I never could when anything with Charlie was concerned.

Pulling away, I stood at the side of the bed. Charlie mewled. Her green eyes were dark with want. Slipping my cut off, I let it drop to the ground before I grabbed the neck of my shirt and pulled it over my head. Charlie sat up, licking her lips as she watched me, her eyes glued to my every move.

The only sound in the room was our breathing and the clink of my belt as I slid my jeans and briefs down my legs and kicked them to the side.

"Holy shit," her eyes widened. "I'm not sure how that thing ever fit inside of me, and now you're," she gulped, her eyes glued to my dick. "Pierced."

Gripping her ankles, I pulled her to the edge of the bed. Running my hands up her silky thighs, I quickly divested the tiny pair of shorts she had on.

I crawled back onto the bed, my dick swinging and weeping to be inside Charlie. Leaning over to the bedside table, I opened the drawer and pulled out a condom.

Charlie laid back in the bed, and with each passing

second, her legs spread a little wider for me. Once I was fully sheathed, I gripped myself at the base and lined myself up with the prettiest cunt I'd ever seen. I'd tried to avoid looking, but I'd failed. If my dick didn't feel like it was going to fall off, I would have gotten on my knees and eaten that pussy until the sun came up. Instead, it would have to wait. I needed to be deep inside of her. Stat.

With one thrust, I was balls deep inside of her. I was in heaven. I had forgotten what it felt like to have her pussy squeezing and fluttering around my dick. Pushing those thoughts aside, I sat back on my haunches, taking Charlie along with me. Her arms wrapped around my neck. Her big, perky tits pressed into me as we both groaned at the new sensation.

"I swear I can feel it," she muttered as she dragged her teeth along the shell of my ear. It seemed Charlie hadn't forgotten how turned on I got when she touched my ears. It was a part of me I never let anyone else touch.

With my hands on her hips, I moved her up and down my shaft as I pushed up from below, knowing I'd nail her g-spot with my metal. Charlie writhed on my lap. Her moves became desperate. I slammed into her over and over again as I nipped and sucked at the skin on her neck. Trying to claim her, even knowing she could never be mine.

"Sin," she cried out my name as her whole body

started to shake. I picked up my pace and swirled my hips to grind against her clit. I needed to feel her come on my dick before letting go.

"Come for me, baby. Let me feel your pussy suck the life out of my dick." Wrapping my arms around her back, I laid her down and threw her legs over my arms. With this new angle, Charlie started to claw at my back. Her legs shook as she let out a long moan. One thumb went to her engorged clit and furiously circled as I pounded into her, holding my release.

With her back arched off the bed, her head thrown back in bliss with her mouth open in a silent scream, Charlie's inner walls clutched at me like a vise grip. Slowing my pace, I unleashed inside of her, letting her milk me and draw out her pleasure with each languid stroke. Only once her limbs failed to hold onto me and she was limp on the bed did I stop my ministrations. Slowly, I pulled out of her. I removed the condom and threw it into the trash can by my bed.

Even with my heart thundering in my chest, I couldn't remember the last time I'd felt this peaceful.

Lighting up a cigarette, I inhaled the smoke deep into my lungs and held it until my chest felt as if it would explode. As I slowly let it all out, Charlie curled into my side. Her arm and leg draped over me as she nuzzled her face into the crook of my neck.

In that moment, I forgot about everything but the

woman in my bed. That was what Charlie did. She made me forget about the world. It was only her and me. That was why I had to give her up in the first place. I couldn't have a distraction. If I did, I could get my brothers and myself killed. That wasn't an option.

Only now that I had tasted her again, I knew it would be next to impossible to give her up.

EIGHT

CHARLOTTE

I WOKE up sore and alone in bed, which wasn't surprising. While Sin was in a motorcycle club, he always lived on a ranch and had to get up early to do his part. It was a strange dichotomy between being a cowboy and a biker, but somehow it managed to suit him.

There was also the fact that I was going to work today, and Sin couldn't be with me. I wasn't sure why, but he informed me that Crow and Dare would be accompanying me.

Not wanting to keep them waiting, I got dressed quickly in a soft linen dress with nude heels. It was the only outfit I'd brought for work. I'd need to swing by my place later to get an outfit or two if they didn't hear back on where this Roach would be.

Putting my hair up in a high ponytail, I put on a light

layer of makeup and called myself done. I'd be busy today with the shipment coming in and didn't need to be all made up. It would likely melt off my face once I was in the storeroom working on cataloging all the items in today's shipment.

I pulled up short when I stepped outside Sin's cabin to find him facing off with two men. He was heated, and they were grinning at him like the cat that ate the canary. I wasn't sure if he heard me or felt my presence, but Sin stiffened and turned to study me. His eyes swept up and down my frame twice before he pointed a finger at each of the men and stalked off in the other direction.

"What was that about?" I asked as I watched Sin disappear into the stables, never once looking back.

"It might have something to do with not being on your protection team," the insanely good-looking and dark-haired man said with a grin. I thought his name was Crow. It was hard to keep all their names straight after only meeting most of them once.

Crossing my arms over my chest, I jutted out my hip. "I do not understand why he can't be either."

"Because Sin is too easily distracted by you. He can be back here monitoring what's happening. We'll be setting up our own cameras in select spots since only two of us are going."

"And you didn't think to ask if it would be okay with me? I'm not sure the owners will be very happy," I huffed. These men. Give them an inch, and they take a mile.

"It's not hooking into their system. Once we're done, we'll remove them, but for now, they're needed. I thought you were on board with our protection." The other man said.

I wanted to snap at them and say I didn't have a choice, but they were only trying to help me. I should be grateful. "Just try to make sure no one else will see the cameras. I won't be the only person there, and people will wonder why cameras in other locations suddenly popped up." Especially the owner of the gallery.

"Not a problem. You won't even know they're there. If anyone tries to get in, they'll be hiding from the cameras that are in plain sight. Ours will catch them."

I nodded and thanked them.

"We should get going before Sin comes back or before you're late. I have a feeling that's very uncharacteristic of you." Crow opened the back door of the SUV sitting outside Sin's place.

"You'd be right." That would be the first indication something isn't right. Still, I didn't like it. They could read me so easily.

"Then let's get you on your way." I slid into the back seat while Dare got behind the steering wheel.

The ride was silent, but that was okay. I didn't have anything to say to them and, for some strange reason, I was nervous. It didn't help that I knew at some point today or tomorrow, my bosses, Randy and Clyde, would show up, and I'd have to make it look as if one or both of these men were shopping for something.

"Don't worry. We know how to behave out in public."

"For the most part," Dare added in.

"Are you both coming in?"

"For now. Once the cameras are set up, one of us will get lost across the street at the coffee shop. If anyone stays around for too long, we'll switch it up."

At least I knew some of the plan. Pulling my keys out of my purse, I unlocked the door and let them inside. They moved in different directions, and I went to sit behind my desk and started up my computer. The system had been updated a couple of years ago, and now I didn't have to wait around for ten minutes before I could log in.

I went through the picture gallery to see what I wanted to pull from storage for the upcoming show. With a list made, I headed back to the storage room. I unlocked the back door and propped it open, only for Dare to slam the door shut.

"Are you trying to get killed? Seriously, have some self-preservation."

"What did I do?"

"You were leaving the door open for anyone to come

in. Do you at least know who will be delivering your art?"

"Yes, of course, I do. It's always the same guys."

"Good." He narrowed his eyes at me. "If it's someone you don't know, don't let them in. You have to be cautious right now." Dare closed his eyes and muttered. "If Sin was here, he'd beat your ass."

"What the fuck are you talking about?"

Dare's eyes slowly opened, and he rolled them. "Not literally. Get a grip. Just be safe for *him*. If anything happens to you, he's going to go berserk on me."

That made me smile. "I feel like you could hold your own against Sin."

"Definitely, but I wouldn't want to if something bad happened to his girl on my watch." He patted my shoulder.

"I'm not his girl," I argued back.

"Both of you are only fooling yourselves. Stop being stubborn and give in. One thing I've learned since joining the Diamond Kings is that our days are numbered, and we never know when our last days are going to be. Let him in before it's too late." Dare gave me a sympathetic smile and then disappeared to wherever he'd come from before.

After two nights of out-of-this-world sex, I couldn't deny our sexual chemistry was phenomenal. Still, I knew there was something Sin was keeping from me. My memory was hazy from the party the other night, but Sin mentioned something about having to give me up. He didn't give me up, though. He cheated, and I dumped his ass. It took years for my heart to mend back together enough for me to even attempt to date again. I knew if I let him in again and he broke my heart, I would never be whole again.

A loud knock on the door broke me out of my revelry. Remembering what Dare said, I called out. "Who is it?"

"Um… it's Dan and Pete. We have your shipment to unload." His tone was confused, and I didn't blame him.

I sheepishly smiled as I opened the door. Dare had locked it again. "I'm sorry, there have been some break-ins in the areas, and I wanted to make sure it was you."

Dan nodded and gave me a soft smile. "I understand, Ms. Hunter. I would never want to do anything that would make you unsafe. We'll keep a lookout for anyone suspicious." He handed me the clipboard that had a list of the items they'd bring in.

"Thanks, Dan. That would mean a lot to me. It can be a kind of scary being here all alone."

"Say no more." He ducked his head and moved back out the way he came. I stood to the side and waited for them to bring in the shipment. I started checking off each item and cataloging it in the system. Once they were gone, I had to open each item and photograph it. It would take me the next few days to finish while also deciding what we'd pull for the show.

"You know, you really shouldn't have the front unlocked if you're going to be back here all day." I jumped at Crow's voice. I was so immersed in my work that I hadn't realized I wasn't alone. "You should at least have someone out there. This doesn't seem like a one-person job."

He was right. It wasn't.

"I'm not usually back here, but this has to be done. Randy or Clyde should come in eventually, and they'll man the front."

Crow crossed his arms over his chest. "It's not safe for you back here all by yourself."

"It's a good thing I'm not by myself now, isn't it?" I arched a brow. "Are you finished setting up your cameras?"

"We are. Let's hope Sin doesn't see the delivery man salivating all over you."

I looked up to where I knew one of the gallery cameras was located. I had no idea where theirs were. "Is he watching?"

"Oh, you bet your sweet ass he'll be watching as soon as we turn the system on," he grinned and then flashed his teeth. "It's killing him not to be here with you."

"Do you really think they'd try to take me here?"

"I wouldn't put it past them to do it anywhere. The

Diamond Kings aren't good guys, but we have standards. Satan's Savages have no qualms about what they do to women. If they know you're here, they'll do anything to get to you."

My entire body stiffened. I wanted to kill Terry for getting me into this mess, even though I had a feeling he was already dead. I hadn't seen the three dead bodies on the ground, but knowing there were bodies at all had me believing one of them could and probably was him.

"Don't worry. That's why we're here." Crow patted me on the shoulder. He turned to start to leave but came back when I called after him.

"You might do bad things, but you're good guys. You wouldn't be here if you weren't, and I wouldn't be at the ranch. So, thank you for looking out for me when you don't have to and for being good… bad guys."

"Not a thing, darlin'."

Several hours later, I was dragging. I'd been hard at work, but it was more than that. The last two nights, Sin kept me awake until all hours of the night with his talented hands, mouth, and cock. I wasn't sure how he was up and out of bed before me each morning, but he was. Maybe he was in his bed taking a nap instead of working or watching me. I highly doubted it, though. I was dead on my feet when Clyde wandered into the back.

"Charlotte, you look a mess. Have you not been sleeping?"

I shook my head and pried another box open. I moved past him to grab the camera and snap a shot at the items.

"Why don't you take the rest of the day off? You do know you can't finish all of this in one day, don't you?" When I nodded, he only smiled and ushered me out of the storage room. "You can continue this tomorrow."

"Thanks, Clyde. Hopefully, I'll get some better sleep tonight."

"I doubt you'll be getting much sleep if I have anything to say about it." A low, gritty voice that I instantly recognized said. My whole body shuddered in revulsion as Roach came out of the shadows.

I tried to push back, but Clyde's hand was like steel on my back. Looking over my shoulder at him, I found him with his head hung. "I'm sorry, Charlotte. I had to. They threatened to burn down the gallery."

"You're in on this. Where are…" I clamped my mouth shut, not wanting to say Crow and Dare's names in case they were in the shadows waiting.

"Oh, I sent them to the café across the street. I convinced them I knew everything and that I'd watch out for you while they got us all some coffee." Clyde looked at Roach. "They won't be gone long. They were highly suspicious. I did what you asked. Now take Charlotte and go."

Roach moved quickly, pulling out a gun and firing it. I screamed, thinking the bullet was meant for me. After several long seconds and feeling nothing, I opened my eyes to find Clyde on the floor with a hole in his forehead.

"Oh my God," I shrieked.

"God's got nothing to do with this. I'm your god now. You'll do everything I say and worship at my feet. Otherwise, I'll make you watch as I shoot your boyfriend, and then I'll cut off your tits and cunt before I do the same to you."

My brain shut down. That was the only reason for what I did next. I lunged at Roach, trying to claw his eyes out, but was stopped short with a fist to the face. I'd never been hit in my life. Falling to the ground, I clutched my cheek. I wouldn't be surprised if my cheekbone was broken.

"I never would have expected you to be so feisty. I like a woman who fights back," Roach laughed as he hauled me off the ground by my ponytail. My feet scrambled on the concrete floor as I tried to pry his hand loose. It felt as if he was going to scalp me.

Crow and Dare came into view. The tears that filled my eyes slipped down my cheeks. I'd been so stupid.

"Let go of her," Crow growled out.

"I don't think so. See, the thing is, she belongs to me, and I plan to use her up until there's nothing left for her to give. When I'm done, you'll find her burned corpse out in the desert." He held me in front of him like a shield. I knew they'd have to shoot me to get to Roach, and even then, it didn't mean he wouldn't kill me and then them.

"Tell Sin I love him and that our time together was too short," I sobbed out as Roach pulled me backward and out into the alley. A white van sat waiting for us with the door open. I was thrown inside, and I didn't care. My life was over. Unthinkable things were going to happen to me, and then I would die. That was how my life would end.

At least I had Sin in my final days—what I wouldn't give to see him one more time.

CROW'S NAME flashed on my screen. Dread started to build in my stomach as I accepted his call. "Talk to me, brother."

"They got her, Sin. Fuck," he shouted. I could hear it echo wherever it was.

I was already exiting the stables when my mouth began to work. "How?"

"Her boss was in on it," he gritted out. "He's dead. Tell me you put a tracker on her this morning," he demanded.

I hadn't seen Charlie awake this morning, but she had laid out what she was going to wear to make sure it didn't have any wrinkles in it, or at least that's what she told me. It didn't matter to me, but it did give me the perfect opportunity to add another tracker to the collar of her shirt.

"Of course, I did," I grunted out as I swung my leg over my bike. Pulling my phone away from my ear, I opened up the app and selected the only tracker I knew she'd have on her. I didn't have time to waste.

My heart sped up as I saw she was on the move and headed out of town.

"She's headed west on I-10. They're almost out of town." I copied a link to the tracker and sent it to Tank. He could relay to everyone where I was headed.

"We're on the move."

Slipping my phone into my vest, I took off with the sun on my back chasing me. I sped down the long drive and hit the road. I wanted to be the first to arrive and take my fury out on Roach for taking what was mine. I didn't give a fuck if there wouldn't be a truce between Satan's Savages and us. Tonight, I would end their President's life.

As I neared the last location from the tracker, I pulled over to the side of the road and checked to see where Charlie was. She wasn't far from where I'd last seen her. It was the middle of nowhere, which was probably why we'd never been able to find Roach on our own.

Back on the road, I gunned it as if the devil himself was chasing after me and keeping me away from my girl.

It didn't take me long to see two brake lights up ahead at the rate I was going. Until that moment, I had forgotten Crow and Dare were in a cage instead of their bikes. I sped up to catch them.

The SUV pulled over and waited for me. I pulled up beside the passenger side and turned off my motor.

"What's the plan?" Dare asked. His eyes were dark with rage.

"No plan. We don't know what we're walking into. It could be a trap knowing we'd find Charlie."

"Or they have no clue she's got a tracker on her and will be completely surprised," Crow added.

"True. I should probably leave my bike here so it doesn't alert anyone." It was too bad they hadn't taken the van where we could have loaded it up.

"I'll send one of the prospects to bring the van and pick it up." Dare was already typing on his phone.

With no time to waste, I left my bike on the side of the road without glancing back. It was then I knew how serious I was about Charlie. This wasn't because she was my ex or a woman. I wouldn't ever let harm come to them. The sickness that was spreading through me at the thought of what might happen to Charlie was because I loved who she was now, the same as I loved her all those years ago.

We parked about a quarter of a mile away and silently crept up to an old, abandoned house. No one would ever look twice at it. I started to wonder if this had been a pit stop and stripped Charlie of her clothes until Crow pointed out a van parked on the side of another building.

It was too quiet, and I didn't like it. We could wait for backup, but I couldn't stop thinking about all the ways Roach was touching my girl.

"Let's circle once to see if we can see or hear anything, and then we move," I directed.

With each step, rage built inside of me until I was a volcano ready to blow.

Dare turned after we made the first pass. "Do you think there's a basement?"

"There has to be. There was no movement inside. Even if they're waiting for us, we would have heard something."

"I'll go through the back. Crow, you take the front. Dare you follow behind. Let the men know we're going in. Count to five when you get there and go in."

They nodded and headed for the front. Pulling my gun out of my waistband, I wasted no time hitting the backdoor and busting through. It was silent for a moment until all hell broke loose. Two men burst out of a door that I would later learn led to the basement at the same time Crow swept in from the front. I shot the first one dead center in the chest. The other went down with a bullet to the head.

I was reaching for the doorknob when Crow gripped

the back of my cut. "We don't know how many are down there."

"I don't care how many are down there. I've got to save Charlie before they kill her, or worse."

It was then we heard the roar of motorcycles. The sound was music to my ears. Two beats later, it sounded like a stampede had been let loose inside the house as all my brothers came rushing in, and they came prepared. More than one guy was ex-military in our club, and they came in handy in times like this. Someone handed me a pair of night-vision goggles with a mask as they moved by. It was hard to tell who with how dark it was.

I placed them on top of my head in case I needed to use them. I knew if it wasn't dark down below, they'd only be a hindrance. Next, I was handed a flash grenade. Yes, my boys definitely came prepared. I should have had a bag packed if this very scenario occurred, but I was too preoccupied with Charlie.

I knew they were all waiting for me to make my move. Counting down from three to one with my fingers, I opened the door and threw the flash grenade down the stairs. After only waiting for a second, I barreled down with my gun drawn and my men trailing behind me.

It was chaos down there. Four men were shouting and covering their eyes, and they aimed at any noise they heard. They swung back and forth, not knowing what to do. They were ill-prepared for our arrival. The men behind me took down each man one by one. It was a sight to see Satan's Savages men dwindle before my very eyes, but I only cared about ending one. I found him in a room at the very back. Roach kept Charlie's back to his front as he held a knife to her throat. Tears slipped down her cheeks as she silently cried.

"You've got something that belongs to me, and I want it back," I growled. I scanned her for injuries. She was a little dirty, there was a mark on her neck, and her wrists were red around the bindings at her wrists. I was grateful she still had on her clothes.

Roach let out a sinister laugh. He sounded like some stupid villain in an old movie as he threw his head back. "She's mine, but I'd be willing to sell her to you for a small price. Let's see." He rubbed the gun against his chin. "Maybe… five million dollars."

I'd pay five billion dollars for Charlie if that was what it took, but I knew Roach would keep coming back for her, and he wouldn't stop until he was six feet under.

"Let her go, and I might think about keeping you alive." There was no chance of that, but I didn't want to risk Charlie getting hurt. Roach seemed to realize that. His grip on her waist tightened as he pressed the tip of his knife to her jugular.

That move made me see red.

"Close your eyes, Charlie," I demanded. She didn't

need to see what was about to happen. It was bad enough that she was here and would have to hear it.

Doing as I asked, Charlie's eyes closed as she bit down on her bottom lip.

"What are you going to do?" Roach laughed, but there was a twinge of nervousness in it this time.

Taking a deep breath, I centered myself and shot.

It all happened so fast and yet in slow motion at the same time as it seemed to do in life and death moments. Charlie screamed and struggled in Roach's hold. His eyes went wide, but my bullet hit dead center in his forehead before he could move. Roach dropped, with Charlie going along with him.

Rushing over, I picked Charlie up and held her to me, breathing her in. "Are you okay?"

"Is it really you, or is this all just a dream?" Charlie sobbed as she buried her face in my chest.

My hands shook as I cut away her bindings. "I'm as real as they come."

"I was so scared," she croaked out.

"I know you were. I was scared too." I pulled her back into my arms and held her to my body. "Come on, let's get you out of here."

"Is it safe?" She murmured into my chest.

"It's all taken care of. You don't have to worry anymore. No one will ever bother you again." I smoothed my hand down her silky brown hair. When she tried to pull away, I held her closer to me. "You don't want to see what's out there."

"Okay." Her word was barely more than a whisper.

I realized then that shuffling her out of the room, up the stairs, and out of the house would take too long. Nothing ever felt so right in my life as when I picked her up bridal style. Charlie squeaked in my arms at the sudden change. "Put your arms around me and keep your head down and eyes closed."

Tiny shivers started, and by the time I had Charlie outside, her body was full-on quaking. Her teeth were chattering, and I knew she was going into shock. There was nothing I could do for her until we made it back to the compound except hold her on my lap and rub my arms over her arm and legs.

"Let's roll out," I directed Dare and Crow as I stalked toward the van that was now parked in front of the house. I would have had someone else drive, but they didn't have their bikes here.

"How is she?" Crow asked as he slipped behind the steering wheel.

"Physically, she's mostly fine, but she's in shock. I'm not sure what her state of mind will be once it wears off. She's not used to this life."

Dare looked back, his eyes softening for a moment as he gazed upon Charlie. "Being kidnapped and sold isn't anything you can prepare for no matter what life you live."

"I wish I could have kept him alive only so I could torture him until he begged me to end his life. Not that I'd give it to him. I'd draw it out and make him die a slow and painful death for ever putting Charlie in danger."

"The ex or Roach?" Dare chuckled. His eyes turned dark at the thought of more spilled blood.

"Both," I growled, making Charlie jump. "Shh, it's okay." I kissed the crown of her head. "You're safe now."

We were almost at the compound when her whole-body shakes stopped, and her body started to stiffen in my arms. I didn't want to try to get her to talk to me with Crow and Dare around. I knew she wouldn't be comfortable, so I tried to comfort her the best way I knew how. I murmured things from our past in her ear in the hope it would take her back to that time and not the present.

"Do you remember the time I took you to the carnival, and we got stuck at the top of the Ferris wheel for two hours? Fuck, you were so beautiful that night. You had your hair pulled up, showing off that long neck of yours I love. After thirty minutes or so of seeing everyone scrambling down on the ground below us, we thought we'd be stuck up there all night. We definitely made the best out of the situation." I breathed her in and smiled. She stilled smelled the same after all these years. "Do you know how hard it was for me not to fuck you while we were alone in the clouds that night? I wanted so badly to take you right then and there. That would have been more special than the backseat of your car."

I hadn't done right by Charlie back then, but I'd do it now. The only thing was I didn't know what the right thing to do was, or maybe I did, and I just didn't want to think about what my life would be like with Charlie gone for good.

It didn't matter what I said, though. Charlie remained stiff in my arms.

Crow pulled the van up to my cabin and left it running as I stepped out with Charlie still in my arms. I cradled her in my arms like a baby as I walked the short distance to my front door and opened it.

I took her into the bathroom, where I sat her on the counter before I started the water in the shower. Having a bathtub at that moment would have been nice. I could have sat down and held Charlie in my arms while I washed away the dirt and hopefully a little bit of the nightmare. That was the first time in all the years I'd lived here that I wished I lived somewhere else.

Moving back to her, I removed her shoes and watched as she scrunched up her toes, retreating from me. "Lift up your arms." My voice was as quiet as a mouse. I didn't want to spook her any more than she already was. Charlie followed my direction and lifted her arms above her head. I removed her shirt and bra, discarding them on the floor. Charlie's arms fell back to her sides as she continued to stare straight ahead.

Lifting her by her hips, I placed Charlie back on the floor and squatted to remove her pants and underwear. I didn't like her body imitating a statue, nor that I didn't know what was going through her head.

I stripped out of my clothes and guided Charlie into the shower and under the water. Squirting some of her body wash into my palm, I lathered it up and ran my hands along her shoulders and down her arms. With each swipe of my hands, she slowly started to relax. I kept my touch light as I glanced the surface of her breasts. I didn't want her to think I wanted anything sexual to happen. My dick knew now wasn't the time and stayed hanging between my legs.

Moving on, I put a dollop of her shampoo in my hand and ran my hands through her hair until it was nice and bubbly. Next, I used her conditioner. Using the pads of my fingers, I massaged her scalp until she was leaning back against me.

She was almost asleep on her feet when I turned her around after rinsing her hair and body off. Turning off the water, I grabbed a towel and dried her off slowly and carefully before I wrapped the towel around her. I quickly dried myself off before carrying Charlie back into the bedroom and sitting her down on my bed. She'd made the bed earlier, which was something I never did. What was the point if you were going to sleep in it again that night?

Pulling the covers back, I brought Charlie with me. Once we were situated with the blankets over her shoulders and the front of her body molded to my front, I ran my fingers through the loose strands of her hair. Her eyes drooped a little more with each circuit until her breaths were shallow. Even in her sleep, I could feel her body jerk as if trying to wake up or fight.

I was prepared to stay up all night to fight the demons in her head or out in the real world. I'd do whatever it took to make Charlie feel safe.

I must have fallen asleep at some point.

The second my eyes popped open, Charlie blinked open her own eyes and ended my world. "I want to go home."

TEN

CHARLOTTE

SIN BLINKED at me sleepily for a moment, as if he couldn't believe the words that came out of my mouth. I couldn't either, but I needed time to think without having him so close or smelling his scent. Everything was muddled, and I needed time to breathe.

He jackknifed in bed and threw the covers off to the side. "Okay, I can spare a day before I have to deal with the aftermath of yesterday."

I watched as Sin stood and walked over to the dresser. The flex of his thigh muscles and the way the globes of his ass moved with each movement had me wanting to take back my next words. "I think I should go alone."

He looked over his shoulder, and his dark eyes lasered in on the way I was clutching the sheet to my chest. His shoulders deflated as he spoke. "Are you afraid of me now?"

"No," I scrambled up on my knees. "I could never be scared of you, but…"

"I should've been at the gallery with you, and for that, I'm sorry. I'll never be able to forgive myself for letting Roach get to you." He hung his head in defeat. I hated it. How could I make him understand?

Wrapping the sheet around me, I moved to stand in front of Sin. "I'm glad you weren't there. If you had been, he probably would have killed you."

Sin scoffed and leaned back against his dresser. It didn't faze him in the least that he was stark naked in front of me. "You underestimate me. He would've been dead, and you never would have experienced being captured."

"I'm fine, Sin."

"Are you?" He shouted, his eyes blazing with equal amounts of anger and sadness. "If you're fine, then why do you want to go home? And why don't you want me to come with you?"

"Because I need time to think, and I can't do that with you near."

He folded his arms over his chest, and it took every ounce of me not to drool over the corded muscles in his arms or the way his chest flexed. "Why not?"

"Because look at you." I waved my hand over the

front of him like I was one of those showcase girls on The Price is Right. "You have the body of a god and the dick of a… I don't even know. A god would be envious of you. It's a lot to overcome."

"I still don't understand, Charlie. I can give you space. I'll sleep at the clubhouse, and you can stay here. Whatever you want."

"What I want is to go back home to my apartment. Alone. Give me a week, and then—"

"A week," he pushed off the dresser and into my space. "What do you need a week for?" Sin moved to pull me to him, but I took a step back. I knew I'd change my mind once I was in his arms and felt his strength around me. His arms fell to his sides. "Why does this feel like I'll never see you again?"

"I'm not saying that."

"But you're also not saying I'm wrong. Talk to me, Charlie," he begged. Sin was not a man who ever begged. He never tried to get me back after I caught him cheating, but now he looked at me with his sad brown eyes that knew they were losing me.

"I'll talk to you in a week. Right now, I need time to… I just need time, Sin, and you need to respect that.

"I do, Charlie. I do, but at the same time, I don't want to let you go. You'll see how much better your life is without me in it."

"Can you have someone else take me home, or do I

need to call an Uber?"

Sin turned and opened a drawer before pulling on a pair of jeans. He tugged them on so hard I thought he would rip the seam. It didn't escape my notice he was going commando as he stormed out of the cabin. While he was gone, I ran to my suitcase and threw on the first thing I saw: a pair of yoga pants and a dark gray t-shirt. I slipped on my pair of boots even though it wasn't the best fashion choice, but I didn't have a lot of options. Before Sin could come back, I threw the rest of my things in the suitcase and zipped it up. I had it waiting by the door when he came back in.

Sin's eyes immediately focused on the suitcase by the door. His jaw hardened when his eyes met mine. "I guess you're ready to go. Rooster will drop you off at home."

"Thank you," I whispered, barely able to get the words out.

He stepped back as I grabbed my suitcase. "If you need anything, you have my number." His words were clipped, and I knew it was impossible to understand why I was doing what I was doing. I barely understood it myself. All I knew was my world had been turned upside down in the last week, and I needed to wrap my mind around everything.

Looking up at him, I saw he'd shut down. I lifted my hand, ready to comfort him, but Sin turned away from my touch. "It's only for a week."

He dipped his head in confirmation but gave no other indication he heard me. I wanted to say more, but I had no idea what I'd say that would ease either of our minds.

"Bye, Sin." I looked over my shoulder, hoping for something more when I shouldn't have. Sin was pissed, and I'd done that to us both.

Rooster was waiting for me out front in the same SUV Sin took me home in a few days ago. Maybe I should have let Sin take me home. Then maybe things wouldn't be so awkward between us. At least Rooster didn't try to make any small talk, even though he kept looking back at me in the rearview mirror every few seconds. I wasn't surprised when he walked me all the way to my apartment door, set my bags inside, and didn't walk away until he heard me lock the door.

A security system beeped at me from beside the front door. I wanted to be mad that Sin had invaded my privacy, but it made me feel safer, so I wasn't too mad.

I stripped out of my clothes as I made my way into my bathroom. A hot bubble bath would hopefully help clear my mind of some of the mess that was going through it. Pouring some lavender and chamomile tea bubbles under the water, I watched as it started to foam up. The smell started to relax me before I even sank into the depths of my bathtub.

The water was a little hot as I dipped my toe inside the steaming water. Slowly sinking inside, I didn't stop until only my head was above the water. Resting my head back, I closed my eyes and placed a washcloth over my face.

My mind drifted to what would become of the art gallery now that Clyde was dead. I didn't even know if Randy was still alive. Maybe they killed him too, or maybe he was in on it as well.

Would I ever be able to go back without always remembering the horrors of yesterday?

If the gallery was gone, what would I do with my life? I could always move away to another city, maybe even New York or Los Anglos, to work in the art field. There were plenty of jobs there compared to Diamond, Texas. But if I left, there would be no Sinclair Matthews where I went.

That was the true conundrum. While I loved Sin with every beat of my heart, I wasn't sure if I was meant to be a part of his life. There was still something he was hiding from me, and if he couldn't open up to me, then there was no real chance for us. Although after today, I might have fucked up everything between us.

Could I accept the life Sin lived? I wasn't sure. I knew very little about it. The only things I did know was that I liked the men he referred to as his brothers, and I loved Sin.

I just wasn't sure if that was enough.

IT WAS COMING up on one week of radio silence from Charlie. Not that I thought she would be calling me or sending me texts, but I hoped I'd hear something. It killed me that I had no idea how she was doing. All I knew was that she hadn't left her apartment since Rooster dropped her off.

At least I knew she was safe. And the only reason I knew that was because when I had her security system set up, I had it added to my phone as well. If she left, an alert would go off on my phone, and so far, nothing.

I might be more worried if the text I'd sent had gone unread, but each night before she went to sleep, or so I liked to think, Charlie would read whatever random text I sent for the day. Only tonight, there'd be no text. I'd been on the road all day. We had a gun run that had us setting off at first light. The drop-off and ride were smooth. I should have enjoyed being on the open road more, but all I could think about was if I'd hear from Charlie at the end of the day.

Tank signaled for us to disembark. There was a little roadside diner where he liked to stop on our way back. It had my lips twitching for the first time since I found out Charlie was taken.

I ordered my usual greasy bacon cheeseburger with a side of fries and a beer. Even though I didn't want to admit it, I looked forward to this dump. Even the rickety old picnic tables that were battered by the wind, sand, and sun after being exposed for at least the last decade.

Tank leaned forward on his elbows with a fry dangling between his fingers. "You seem a little lighter than you have all week."

"Fuck off," I chuckled. "The road always calms me."

"That's why I brought you on this run. I didn't need you, but I figured you needed this."

He wasn't wrong, and I appreciated Tank getting me out of my head, at least for a little while. Nothing else had worked all week.

An engine roared, catching all of our attention, but we were too late. The door on a nondescript white van flew open two seconds before shots rang out.

"Get down," I shouted. I wasn't sure if this was meant for us, but doing it in a public place where all these innocent people could get hurt wasn't how it was supposed to go. Pulling the Glock from my waistband, I ducked behind the table and shot at the van as it sped by.

It all happened so fast. I was emptying my clip one second, and the next, it felt like I'd been hit in the chest by a bus. I was thrown onto my back and staring up at the sun. Its bright light blinded me as I tried to catch my breath, but it wouldn't come. With each attempt, it became harder and harder for air to fill my lungs.

A shadow blocked the bright sunshine before Tank's face came into view. "Fuck, Sin," he growled out. "Call fucking 911. Now," he shouted. I'd never heard Tank sound out of control, but in that moment, I became worried.

"What happened?" I croaked out as black spots started to dot my vision.

"You've been shot." He looked down and then back up at my face. "I think it hit your lung, but don't worry, an ambulance will be here soon to fix you."

"No hospital." I barely got the words out. I wasn't even sure if he heard me or not.

"Fuck, man. The doctor we use can't patch you up, and I'm not risking you dying. We were sitting here eating our dinner doing nothing wrong when those assholes shot you."

This would put an even bigger spotlight on us with

the police, and it would be all my fault because I was the stupid motherfucker who got shot.

I was shaking my head when my vision started to grow black. It was impossible to suck in a breath. It felt like I was drowning in my own body.

Loud noises surrounded me, and then everything went silent.

It must have been raining. Water was dripping on my hand, arm, face, everywhere, it seemed. I tried to place where I last was. I didn't remember rain in the forecast. I would have made sure the horses were in the stable if I had known.

"Sin." My name was a soft cry from the most beautiful mouth to ever exist. It was then I knew I must be dreaming or dead. There was no way Charlie was here, wherever I was. It was most definitely Hell. Heaven wasn't for the likes of me, and my torturous afterlife existence would be hearing Charlie whisper my name like a prayer over and over again until the end of time.

"I know it hurts, but I need you to come back to me," she whimpered.

The pain didn't matter. I'd do anything for Charlie. Even come back from the dead.

"I love you, Sin. Did I tell you that? No, I don't think I did," she rushed out. "But I do. I love you more than anything, and I'll prove that to you once you open your eyes."

Like her words had a direct link to my body and soul, my eyes opened. Charlie's long brown hair was a tangled mess. Her face was streaked with dried tears, but she'd never looked more beautiful.

"Charlie." Even though I said her name, no sound came out. My throat was dry as fuck. My hand lifted to touch her sweet face, but it did nothing more than twitch at my side.

"Sin?" she shrieked so loud I was surprised the windows didn't break, or at least my eardrums.

Soft hands cupped my cheeks as Charlie leaned over me. Tears cascaded down her cheeks and splattered against my forehead, chin, and lips.

"Don't cry."

"What?" She leaned forward with her ear right over my lips. "Say it again."

"Don't cry." Why weren't my words coming out of my mouth? Nothing was working like it was supposed to.

"It's okay. You don't have to talk." Charlie picked up

my hand and held her to her mouth before kissing my knuckles.

Taking in my surroundings, all I saw were white walls and lights. How was she even here?

"The guys are in the waiting room. They only allow one person in the room at a time, and they all thought you'd want to see me when you woke up." She bit her bottom lip. "I hope that's okay."

It was more than okay. I'd much rather wake up to her face than their ugly mugs any day of the week.

I nodded my head, or at least I thought I did. "I'm happy you're here."

Charlie's eyes widened, and a smile brightened her face. "There you are. Are you in pain?" I shook my head even though the right side of my chest burned with more pain than I'd ever experienced before. "I'm going to go get the doctor and let him know you're awake."

"Not yet." I swallowed. My throat felt like it was coated with shards of glass. "How?"

"How did you get here?"

That wasn't what I was asking, but I went along with it and nodded.

"You were eating lunch when there was a drive-by shooting, and you got hit. An ambulance took you to a nearby hospital, and then they brought you here." Her chin started to tremble. "That was yesterday."

Fuck, I'd been out since yesterday.

"I'm fine." I didn't sound fine, but I'd fake it until I made it.

"You better be." Wrapping her arms around my shoulders gently, Charlie rested her head on my shoulder. "I just got you back."

I had to wonder if she was only here until I got better and would then disappear. Once I could speak properly, I'd bring up why she felt the need to leave in the first place.

"I'll be back with the doctor. They can get you something for the pain."

I guess I wasn't fooling her.

I nodded and closed my eyes. I'd just rest them until she was back.

"ARE YOU COMFORTABLE?" I asked as I fluffed the pillow behind Sin's head.

"How can I not be? You've put ten different pillows on my bed." He chuckled lightly.

"I may have gone a little overboard, but you needed more than the two pancakes you called pillows before." I smoothed my hand through his hair and watched as Sin closed his eyes. He'd overdone it today. He'd been home for all of a day, and Sin had already gone to the stables to check on the horses even after the doctors told him he needed to take it easy. I wasn't sure taking it easy was in the man's vocabulary.

"Are you tired? I can go get some groceries for dinner and let you rest."

Sin caught my hand and held it against his chest. "I

want you right where you are. The girls can cook dinner and bring us a plate."

I knew he was right, but I liked cooking. It helped me when I was stressed. If I was going to stay, maybe now would be the time to get some answers.

Lying down on my side, I wrapped my arm around his waist and settled my head on his good shoulder. "Is this okay?"

"Better than okay. I wouldn't have you anywhere else except straddling me, riding my dick." His good hand ran down the length of my hair and landed on my ass. His other arm was in a sling to keep him from moving his arm and not tearing out the stitches.

I laughed. "I don't remember your doctor clearing you for sex."

"My dick is in no way affected by me getting shot. In fact, it's a good two and a half feet away. He's working just fine down there."

"No one said your dick doesn't work. It's the strain of sex that might prolong your recovery."

"That's why I'll let you be on top and do all the work." I could hear the smile in his voice.

Sin wasn't a lazy lover. He was enthusiastic to the nth degree. He was as a teenager and even more so now. Not that I was complaining, but I knew he couldn't just sit back and enjoy the ride.

I curled my body into his and spoke before I chickened out. "Can I ask you something?"

"You can ask me anything." His voice rumbled from his chest.

"I know there's more to it than you let on about why everyone knew my name when I first showed up here."

There was a beat of silence before he spoke. "That doesn't sound like a question. More of a statement."

Lifting up on my elbow, I looked down at him. Sin's eyes were directed at the ceiling. "I want to know why they knew of me."

"Are you sure you want to know this?" His jaw ticked, and I knew he didn't want to tell me what I wanted to know, but he would.

"Yes, more than anything," I whispered.

"I got drunk one night not long after I'd been patched in and spilled everything. I told them all about you. When they asked why we weren't together anymore, I laid it all out there. The men said I did the right thing, while the women called me stupid."

"How was cheating on me the right thing to do?" I snapped. Maybe I didn't want to know how they knew about me.

Sin shook his head and then landed his eyes on me. They held so much sadness in them. "I didn't cheat on you."

"I think I remember the events correctly." I sat up and

crossed my legs to sit beside him. My eyes narrowed into slits as I spoke. "Don't lie to me, Sin, or I'll leave, and I'll never come back."

His jaw hardened at my ultimatum as he kept his eyes locked on me. "I'm not lying. I made it look like you caught me in the act. I knew I couldn't just break up with you. I needed you to hate me, and the best way to do that was for you to think I was fucking some other girl."

"Why would you do that?" I scooted back on the bed and wrapped my arms around my middle.

"Because I knew what you wanted out in the world. You wanted to go to college and have a career, and I wanted the exact opposite. My life in the Diamond Kings would have only hindered your progress. I knew this life wasn't for you, so I staged it so you would walk in at the perfect moment."

There was so much to digest from what he'd just confessed. His words weren't what I was expecting. I thought I was boring in bed, and he wanted someone more enthusiastic or some shit like this. Not that he didn't want to hold me back.

"I…" I had no idea what to say.

"You wouldn't have accepted that I wanted to break up, and I couldn't think of any other way. I knew I had to let you go for you to pursue your dreams and to keep you safe."

"You have no idea what you doing that did to me. I

thought I was worthless for so long." I picked at my cuticles, unable to look at him. All the feels from a decade ago rushed back to me. Unworthy of love and that I would never be enough for any man. "It made me choose the wrong guys for years to come. All because you couldn't be truthful with me."

"I'm sorry, Charlie." He reached out and cupped my knee, but I jerked it away. "I only wanted to give you the best life possible."

"You shouldn't have made that decision without me. It wasn't fair to me." I tightened my hold around myself, feeling like I could fall apart at any second. Building the strength to see the truth in his eyes, I finally tilted my head up to catch his gaze. "And what about now? Are you going to pull the same shit again when one little bad thing happens?"

"There's no way in hell I will sacrifice you again. I'm not strong enough. Who's to say my life won't become too much for you, or you'll start to resent me for the shit that you've already been through and leave me?"

I was already shaking my head. "I don't blame you for what happened. How could I? What happened to me is all on me. I chose the wrong guy for the millionth time. You're the one who saved me."

Sin sat up higher in his bed with a wince. I tried to adjust his pillows, but he was having none of it as he pushed my hand aside. Shit was real now. This is what our lives would be like together. I knew if we couldn't get through this, we wouldn't last.

He reached out and pulled me closer to him. Once my crossed legs were flush to his side, Sin wrapped his arm around my waist. His thumb found a patch of skin and slowly moved back and forth. "I'll save you a million times over again, but I have to warn you. This life is dangerous, and while I'll die to keep you safe, danger will be brought to your doorstep more than once. I cannot drag you into this world without you knowing the consequences."

I wanted so badly to curl into a ball to protect myself, but I knew Sin would never hurt me intentionally again. I understood why he did what he did all those years ago. Did I like it? No, but that was in the past, and all we could do was be open and honest with each other.

"We should have had this conversation ten years ago."

"You were too young to understand the ramifications of what my life would bring. I'm still not sure you grasp my life with my brothers. I would die for them the same I would die for you. They became the family I longed to have for so long."

Sin never talked much about his parents. I tried to keep myself away from them as much as possible back in high school. I knew they were both drunks who loved to fight and trash the house. The cops were called on them regularly. His parents never paid any mind to him. He was a nuisance in their lifestyle of trying to be constantly fucked up. He was lucky to find food to eat in the house. The school provided all of his meals with their free meal program when he was in school.

I needed to be closer to him. Unfolding my legs, I slipped down the bed and rested my head on his shoulder. A spot that was starting to feel like home to me. I knew nothing could ever hurt me here. Tilting my head up, I buried my nose in the crook of his neck and breathed in. Sin was my favorite scent in the whole world, and I never wanted to give him up.

"I'm glad you got the family you've always yearned for." I pressed a kiss to his collarbone. "I want to be included, to be a part of it. You're right, I don't know what I'm getting myself into, but I can tell you that the thought of never seeing you again sends thousands of daggers through my heart."

Sin's arm around me moved to press me further into him. "While I love what you're saying and want that more than anything, I'm not sure I believe it."

My body stiffened, and I tried to sit back up so I could see him better. Sin's one arm held me firmly in place. I tried to peer up at him, but all I saw was the underside of his jaw. He wasn't making this easy on me. "What do you mean you don't believe me?"

"Tell me why you needed a week to yourself," he gritted out.

"Because I was overwhelmed, and it's hard to think straight when I'm near you. I was trying to wrap my head around everything that happened at the gallery." I ran the tip of my finger in loops over his chest. "That one of my bosses and possibly the other was in on me being taken. I watched him die right in front of me, and I needed to process what that would mean for me."

"And what does that mean?" He loosened his grip on me. I could have moved, but I stayed where he wanted me.

"I'm still not sure. I thought about how I could move somewhere else to work, but the thought of losing you stopped that line of thinking. I don't know what will happen to my work, but I do know that I want to be with you now that I know the truth." My hand stopped moving, and I stared at the sling holding his other arm. "I knew you were hiding something from me."

"I didn't see the point in telling you if you were only going to be here for a short time," he grunted.

"Do you want me here?" My words came out in barely more than a whisper. I held my breath as I waited for his answer.

"More than anything. Fuck Charlie, I love you more now than ever before. I wanted to tear the world apart when they told me Roach had you. With each passing second that I thought something might have happened to you, I died a little. I'm not sure if I would have been able to go on if he had killed you with his selfish hands."

"I'll admit I was in shock afterward, but I'm perfectly fine now. You saved me just like I knew you would."

He huffed. "Full disclosure because I don't want any more secrets between us." I nodded. I wanted the same. "I put a tracker in the collar of your shirt that morning before I left. There were others in a few of your belongings. If I hadn't had that tracker on you, I wouldn't have found you in time or until Roach made sure I found you."

His words sent a shiver down my spine. I had wondered how Sin had found me, but I'd never thought too much about it until now. Leaning up on one elbow, I caressed his stubbly cheek with my other hand. "I don't care how you did it. I'm just thankful you saved me."

"I'm not sure I'll ever be able to let you leave me without one. I could pretty it up with a piece of jewelry, but the thought of something else happening to you while you're not by my side will always eat away at me. I should have—"

"How were you to know?" I stopped him. I could see the guilt eating away at him from the inside when all of this was my fault. "You couldn't, and you were doing what I asked of you. I didn't understand the repercussions of my choice. If I had known, I would have stayed here safe in your bed."

I watched in fascination as his tongue peeked out and slipped along his lower lip. "I like you in my bed."

"Good, because I plan to be here for a long time to come." I pecked him on the lips and smiled. "That is if you'll have me."

"I'm never letting you go. Now bring those lips back down here and let me taste you. It's been far too long, and I'm starved for the taste of you.

I couldn't deny him. I wanted to fall into Sin just as badly as he wanted me.

Brushing my lips across his, I relished in the feel of him. It had been too long. Sin's hand cradled the back of my head as he swept his tongue into my mouth and tasted me. I moaned into his mouth. Hooking my leg over his hip, I pressed my body further into his and started to move my hips.

Using my head, Sin angled to get a better angle and deepen our kiss. With each passing stroke of his tongue, I felt my life becoming whole once again. I was always meant to be in Sin's arms and his bed.

We broke apart, our noses touching as we panted for breath. "Fuck, I missed you and your taste. Now, let me taste your sweet pussy. I want to see if it's as good as I remember."

"Sin, you're hurt," I protested lightly. A week was too long without his mouth on every single inch of me.

"Don't deny that, but I can still taste you. Take off your clothes and then come sit on my face. My tongue is working perfectly fine."

Sitting up on my knees, I flung my t-shirt off and had my shorts and panties down my legs in a heartbeat. I sat down and shimmied them the rest of the way off before I stood on the bed and smiled down at Sin. "Are you sure about this?"

"I've never been more sure about anything in my entire life." He gripped my ankle as if I was going anywhere when all I wanted was to feel his mouth on my most sensitive place. His brown eyes were black with lust as he stared up at me. "Now, let me eat your pussy."

I moved to stand with my feet on each side of his head, then lowered myself onto my knees while holding the headboard. I hovered above him until he leaned forward and swiped his tongue through my folds. That one simple movement had me primed and ready to go. Leaning my forehead on the headboard as I held on, my eyes caught on Sin's. He was staring up at me like I was his world, and he'd do anything for me. And I knew it to be true.

Unable to break our eye contact, I held on for dear life as his tongue ran up and down my slit and then swirled around my clit. His hand ran up my thigh and gripped my ass cheek. I rocked back and forth, taking every ounce of pleasure his talented tongue bestowed upon me. When his lips circled around my bundle of nerves and sucked, I nearly flew off the bed. My fingernails dug into the wood of the headboard as I tried to keep eye contact. Just the way Sin looked at me had me so close to tumbling over the edge. When he bit down on my clit, I lost it. My entire body went ramrod straight as I shook from the pleasure. Sin's tongue continued to lightly swirl around to draw out my orgasm. It was one of the best in my life, and he had simply done it with only his tongue.

I slumped against the headboard and then slowly moved to lie down beside Sin. "That was amazing," I sighed.

He hummed deep in the back of his throat. "You taste just as good as I remember." His arm started to push my body on top of him. "Now, I need you to ride my dick fast and hard. Pull me out, baby."

I couldn't deny how badly I wanted Sin to fill me with his big, beautiful cock. Slipping my hand inside his sweatpants, I pulled him out and licked the moisture at his tip. "Are you sure you don't want my mouth?"

"As talented as your mouth is, I want to feel that tight as fuck pussy strangle my cock when you come again."

That was fine with me. I'd suck his cock later.

Straddling his waist, I smiled. I liked being on top

and watching Sin's face morph into raw lust as I rubbed my wet core along his length.

His hips thrust forward, and he was deep inside of me in one move.

With one hand resting on his stomach, I laughed. "You're impatient."

"And you're so damn beautiful I couldn't help myself. I had to be inside of you. The way your cunt clenches around me when I'm deep inside of you is utterly addictive."

My hips started to move all on their own. The feel of his metal running along that magical spot inside of me had me close to combusting. Sin's piercing was a work of magic.

Nothing had ever felt as good as when Sin was sliding in and out of me with my core stretched around him. It made every inch of my body alert and extra sensitive.

I massaged my aching breasts with my free hand, pinching and rolling my nipples. I loved the way Sin watched every action with rapt attention. His hips rolled underneath mine, and his fingers dug into the flesh on my hip.

"Ride me harder, baby. Don't stop touching yourself. You're driving me mad."

Quickening my pace, I slipped my hand down my taut stomach and between my legs. I was a sopping mess. Gliding my fingers through the wetness, I collected the moisture and circled my clit once. Electric shocks filled my entire body, making me convulse around his cock. Sin moaned deep and low, spurring me on. I wanted to watch and hear him come undone. There was something different from this vantage point, or maybe it was that *we* were different from the last time we were joined. Either way, I wanted to memorize tonight, so I could pull it up when times get tough because I knew they would.

Sin's hand ran down my ass cheek and to our connection. I rode him harder, never taking my eyes off him. When I felt him nudge my other entrance, I pushed back, wanting more.

"Fuck, you're perfect for me. Soon I'm going to fill this ass with my cock, and you'll to go out of your mind." His voice was gravelly and pure, raw sex. "Tell me you love me."

"I love you," I moaned, moving my hips and fingers faster.

"I love you, too. You're mine now, Charlie." He punctuated it with a deep thrust of his hips.

I was on sensory overload. So full of Sin. His body, love, and soul.

My entire body shook as white-hot heat engulfed me from head to toe. I went blind for a moment, and when I came back to myself, Sin stilled deep inside me. His face was awash with pleasure. The groan that came out of him nearly had me orgasming again. It rumbled through his whole body as his eyes blazed up at me.

I wanted nothing more than to lie on top of him, close my eyes, and fall asleep, but I knew I couldn't do that. Not with Sin hurt. I was sure he wouldn't say a word to the pain, but I wouldn't risk it.

Leaning down, I kissed him slowly and softly. Our tongues tangled together in a sensual dance. I could have kept kissing him all night.

Slowly, I lifted myself off him and broke our kiss. Moving to lie down, I snuggled into Sin's side. Every inch of my front was plastered to him, and it wasn't enough. As if he felt the same way, Sin slowly rolled to his side, my cheek resting over the pounding beat of his heart as my legs tangled with his. I wrapped my arm around his waist, holding myself to him.

I breathed in his clove and sandalwood scent mixed with sweat. I never wanted tonight to end. It was perfect—until it wasn't.

I was close to falling asleep when I felt wetness start to seep out of me and run down my leg.

I was suddenly very awake. My eyes widened in horror. "We didn't use protection."

Sin shifted back until he could look down at me. "Nothing will ever come between us again for the rest of our lives."

I didn't want to ruin the mood, but I had no idea how many women Sin had been with, and I didn't want to know. Still, the thought that any of those women could have an STD, which in turn might give me one, didn't settle well with me.

"Sin, this is something we should talk about. What if I wasn't on birth control?"

"But you are because I saw your pill pack in my bathroom when you were here before. Although I have to say." He placed his hand on my stomach, his fingers spread wide. "I wouldn't mind planting my seed in you and watching it grow."

Another thing we needed to talk about. It was sweet. Sin was being sweet, but I wasn't sure this life was meant for babies and children. We hadn't even discussed if we wanted kids yet. I guess I now knew Sin wasn't opposed.

He sighed, which made him seem to sink further into the pillow. "What is it, Charlie? Talk to me."

I bit my bottom lip, hating having to bring this up. "What about diseases?"

"I'm clean. The doctor cleared me when I was at the hospital. Are you worried about giving me something?" He smirked.

At least he wasn't upset with me for bringing it up. "No, I don't think so, but I guess I didn't really know Terry all that well, did I? I should probably get tested before we do that again."

He nodded, his eyes drooping. I'd worn him out. This was all too much for him. "Tomorrow," he muttered sleepily.

I snuggled deeper, tucking my head under his chin. The heat from our bodies and the soft sound of Sin's breathing lulled me to sleep.

This was where I was meant to be.

Now and forever.

EPILOGUE

Sin

"ARE you sure you should be up on a horse?" Charlie looked over at me with worried eyes.

"I'm fine. I thought it might do us both some good to get out and enjoy the fresh air." Little did she know there was a surprise waiting for her. I also wasn't lying. I needed out of my cabin. Charlie had been firm. There was to be no sex after our initial time when I got home from the hospital.

It had been a long two weeks.

"Where are we going?"

"I thought it would be nice to go by the creek." I patted my saddlebag.

"Oh," her eyes lit up. "Did you pack us a lunch?"

"And when would I have done that?" She'd been by my side almost every second of the day. I was lucky enough to get in a phone call with Layla to get something together for us in a short period of time. "I did arrange it, though. Does that give me any points?"

Charlie smiled brightly. "You get all the points for setting this up." She lifted her face to the sun. "This was a good idea. The sun feels good on my skin."

"I'd be happy to lay you out naked and help all of your skin get a little vitamin D."

"You're so magnanimous."

We both laughed, which felt good.

Two minutes of riding later, she looked over at me. "Are you really okay?"

"I'm fine, Charlie. I wouldn't be out here otherwise." And I wasn't going to do anything to prolong her ban on sex. Who could blame me for being tired and falling asleep after some mind-blowing sex?

"I'm just worried. You almost died." Her pink lips turned down, and I hated it.

I was pretty sure I did die, but I wasn't going to tell her that.

"How about if I feel any pain, I'll let you know?"

"And if you get tired," she added.

"And that as well. I promise. Let's just enjoy today out of the house."

It only took us a few more minutes to get to the creek. Instantly, I relaxed at the sound of the water. I loved how peaceful it was here.

Charlie dismounted. I could also see her body relax with each step she took toward the water. "Did I tell you how much I love it here?"

I watched as she started to shed an article of clothing as she walked. It was a good thing everyone knew to keep a wide berth of this place. Each uncovered inch of her golden skin had my dick getting harder by the second.

Following Charlie's lead, I stalked toward her while removing my clothes. I thought it would be harder to convince her, but I guess not.

"You look beautiful with the sunlight on your skin." I wrapped my arms around her waist and kissed up her neck.

Looking at me over her shoulder, Charlie met her mouth to mine. "This place is almost as magical as your dick." She swayed her ass until my dick was planted between her legs.

"I'm glad you think so because it's ours."

"I like that we have a special place. We should come here more often."

"What would you say if we were here all the time?"

"What are you talking about?" She turned around

and pressed her tits into my chest as she looked up at me.

My hands slid up her back, holding her to me. "The guys thought they'd surprise us by giving us the cabin. This view could be yours if you want it."

"Who wouldn't?" She looked around, her smile growing even larger. "They're really giving us all this?"

"My brothers are good to me, and they'll be good to you as well."

"They already were. They came with you to save me. I want to see the inside once you fuck me out here in our front yard."

Our front yard. I liked the sound of that.

"I'm happy to oblige. Give me a second." I pressed a hard kiss to her still smiling lips. I backed away and moved to grab the blanket out of my saddlebag. Spreading the blanket on the ground, I motioned Charlie to come to me. "I like it when you look at me that way."

"What way?" She giggled.

"Like you want to devour me and me to do the same to you."

Charlie stepped up to me and ran her hands up my stomach and around my neck, making sure her hands skirted the area where I'd been shot. She acted as if I would shatter on contact if she touched my wound. "I can't help it when you look so damn good walking around and all your muscles rippling. I think this area should be a no clothes allowed zone."

"I can agree with that. Get on down on your hands and knees, and stick that perfect ass of yours in the air." I slapped her ass and moved her into position. My dick was weeping to be inside of her after two weeks.

Gripping the base of my cock, I ran length through her dripping folds. "Has this cunt missed me?"

"Yes," she whimpered. "So bad. Fill me up, Sin."

Lining up at her entrance, I gripped her hip with my free hand and slammed inside. We both moaned when my balls slapped against her pussy.

"I love you, Charlie. Don't ever forget that." I ran my hand up her spine and held her at the nape of her neck.

She looked over her shoulder as best as she could with my hold on her. "I love you, too."

Her words spurred me on. I couldn't hold back even if I wanted to. Knowing Charlie loved me like I loved her was still hard to believe. That she was choosing to spend the rest of her days with me was unfathomable, but I wasn't going to object. I needed her like I needed air to breathe. I wasn't sure how I'd functioned the last ten years of my life without her in it.

My hips slapped against her juicy ass. The sound and the way Charlie pushed back against my every thrust had me close to losing myself. "Fuck, Charlie, let me feel your pussy choke my dick. I need you to come now."

Letting go of her nape, I wrapped my arm around her chest and pulled her up until her back was flush to my front. Running my hand down her front, I felt her body start to shake. The muscles in her stomach trembled beneath my touch as I skated my hand down further. My fingers slid through the wetness that was gathering, and using my thumb, I pressed her clit and slowly started to rub circles.

Charlie angled her head, letting me see as the rapture started to take over. I'd never seen anything more beautiful than when she came. Her entire face was one of awe as she came undone against me.

Crashing my mouth to hers, I ate up her scream and moans as her body bucked against mine. The feel of her pussy gripping my cock like it never wanted to let go was my undoing. I buried myself deep inside and let her cunt milk me over every last drop and thought I had while I ate at her mouth. If I could spend the rest of my life kissing this woman, I would. To have my mouth on her twenty-four-seven would be a dream I would work toward every day of my life.

Only once Charlie was slumped back against me did I pull out slowly. I laid her gently down on the blanket and then covered her with half my body as I lay on my side. Charlie ran her fingertips up and down my arm as we slowly came down. It was an otherworldly experience, and I knew each time with my girl would only get better and better with time. We had so much we needed to catch up on.

Charlie giggled, making me look down at her.

"What's got you laughing?" I kissed the top of her head as I waited for her answer.

"My heart is still pounding so hard in my chest. It feels like it's going to burst." She let out a contented sigh. "I'm so happy. I'm not sure I ever want to leave this spot."

"We don't have to. We can make this ground sacred, and we can come out here morning, noon, and night for me to fuck you until we're both spent and can no longer move."

Charlie nuzzled her nose into my shoulder. "I like the sound of that." She kissed my shoulder, and I could feel her lips spreading across my skin. "Did they really give us that cabin?"

"I wouldn't lie to you. They thought it would be nice for us to have a little more privacy, and no one was using it, anyway." I had a feeling if any of the others ever settled down, they'd want to move further out onto the ranch. Our spot was perfect. No one could see us from the clubhouse or the other cabins.

"I haven't even seen inside of it, but I already love it. I could live out here under the sun and stars." She extended her arm and ran her hand over the grass.

We hadn't discussed living arrangements, but she

knew I needed to be at the ranch. It was where I worked and where my brothers were. Still, if she was willing to live in my small ass cabin, she'd be happy with this one.

"What do you say I give you the tour?"

"Have you been in it before?"

"Been in it? I helped build it. I've put my blood, sweat, and tears into it." I disengaged and helped Charlie up to stand. "Let's go see your new home."

Charlie hugged herself to me, looking up at me with wonder in her emerald green eyes. "It doesn't matter where I live as long as I'm with you."

"Good, because I'm never letting you go. If you try to run from me, I'll tie you to the bed."

Her brows kicked up. "Oh, is that a promise? I might have to try and make a run for it."

"You don't have to run for me to tie you up, baby. I'll do whatever you want to your body. All you have to do is say the word, and I'll make every one of your fantasies come to life."

"You already have." She leaned up and kissed me like she was starved for my lips. I felt the same way. I didn't want to be apart from her for even a second. Charlie broke away, panting, and smiled up at me. "I guess I'll have to come up with more."

Taking her hand in mine, I guided us to the front of the cabin and stopped at the keypad by the door. Each cabin had a keypad lock since it was easier than keeping a key for each place. There was a master code that only a couple of us knew, and then there was a separate code for each domicile. I tapped in the number and heard Charlie gasp before she pressed her naked front to my back. Her arms came around me from behind.

"You remembered our first time." Her words were breathy and full of awe.

"I haven't forgotten a single thing about you, Charlie. You've always been the one for me even when I was being stubborn and fighting myself on it." I held one of her hands as I slowly opened the door with my other. "Welcome to your new home."

Charlie peeked around me. The second she laid eyes on the inside, they went wide. She looked up and me and then back inside. "This is ours? You help build this?"

"Yes, and yes," I chuckled. The cabin wasn't as fancy as I was sure some of the places Charlie had seen. She grew up with money. Lots of it, and her house was as close to a mansion as they got in Diamond, Texas. Still, my chest swelled with pride as she looked on with utter fascination.

"I wasn't sure what I was expecting besides a good view, but this is beautiful inside and out."

I understood. The rest of the cabins were all a single room except for the bathroom. This cabin wasn't a mansion, but it was huge compared to the other cabins. It was two stories tall. The bottom floor had a real kitchen with a separate dining room. Both rooms had a big window looking out onto the ranch. The living room faced the creek and had another huge window. You could almost hear the water just by looking at it. A small bathroom was tucked under the stairs that led up to a loft. The entire upstairs was the bedroom and a full bathroom.

"What's up there?" Charlie pointed to the stairs.

"That's our bedroom. Do you want to see it?" I was already dragging her up the stairs before she could answer.

"Sin," she cried out as we set foot at the top of the stairs. "This is… I have no words." There were big windows on all four walls, making it feel like you could see the entire ranch from up there. Everyone had been busy while I'd been recovering. The place was now fully furnished. It had sat empty for the last few years after we built it. From top to bottom, all the furniture was done in a dark brown and fit with the cabin vibe. The lamps by the bed looked to be made out of intertwined tree limbs at the base.

"There's even a fireplace," she gushed as she spun around in circles. "This is all so perfect. How am I ever going to thank them?"

"Just telling them thank you will be enough. They didn't do it for any other reason than they want us happy."

"I'm going to be beyond happy here. This place is more than I could have ever imagined." She skipped off to the bathroom, stopped at the entry, and squealed. "Think I need a bath now."

My brows furrowed. A bath? While the bathroom was nice, there wasn't but a shower in the room. "What are you talking about?" I asked as I moved up behind her. Sitting in front of the window now sat a deep soaking tub with a small table sitting beside it.

"That wasn't here before," I mumbled as I took in the candles scattered throughout the room and the plush towels that sat on the vanity counter.

"It's like this place was made just for us."

Deep down, when we were building it, I think we were all making it something out of our dreams, but now it was a reality. Everyone had gone above and beyond for us and did more than I imagined.

"Why don't you get the water going? I'm going to bring in the lunch that was prepared for us. I'll feed you while you soak."

Charlie turned and ran her hands up my chest. Her hand lightly skimmed where I'd been shot. She was getting better and less timid about it. At least she let me fuck her. "That tub is big enough for two. Why don't you join me?"

"Did you really think I would let you sit in there all

by yourself? I want to feel your silky skin all wet against mine as we slide together."

"I like the sound of that." She bounced up and down. "I'm going to explore a little more while it fills up."

Pulling her to me, I held her ass in both hands and squeezed. "Have at it." Leaning down, I ran my nose up the column of her neck. "I can't wait to be inside of you again."

"God," she moaned. "How can a few simple words make me so wet?"

I chuckled. "Because you're as hungry for me as I am for you." My dick grew hard against her stomach. "Get that water started."

It was hard to break away from Charlie, but somehow, I managed. I moved quickly down the stairs and out the front door. I was a man on a mission to get back inside his woman and to feed her. Picking up the blanket and our clothes, I balled them up and moved over to where Brimstone was grazing on some grass. I rubbed along his side until I reached my saddlebag. I pulled out our food and a carrot for each of the horses. I threw Trixie's over in her direction and held Brimstone's out for him. He took it happily. "Be a good boy." I patted his neck.

I could hear the water was still running as I headed back upstairs. I was still in awe at everything the club had done for us. I was only planning to show Charlie the cabin and let her decorate it as she was fit. To walk inside and have everything done for us was more than I could have asked. Everyone had been busy while I'd been convalescing.

Charlie was leaning over the tub, pouring something inside, when I walked into the bathroom. "What a pretty sight to come home to."

"Sin," she giggled, turning around. "I'd ask if that was a banana in your pocket, but since you're standing buck naked in front of me, I can see plain as day. It's your big cock aimed my way."

"Yes, it is." I dropped the food on the table beside the tub. "Just the thought of you gets me hard, let alone seeing you bent over." I to take her again wanted so badly, but I also wanted her to enjoy our new place. I knew I didn't have Charlie in my bed for a limited amount of time.

I hungrily watched as she stepped inside the water and slowly sank into its depths. She turned her head slowly to look back at me.

"Are you going to join me, or are you going to just stand there and watch? I mean, I wouldn't be opposed to a little show while I enjoy this amazing bathtub." One brow lifted as if to entice me.

"If you want a show, all you have to do is ask. I'll do whatever you want." I ran my hands down my torso and along the deep V that Charlie loved so damn much. I imagined my fingers where her tongue as I trailed down my obliques.

"How are you so in shape? I've never seen you work out." She licked her lips.

"There's a gym in the clubhouse that I use two or three times a week, plus there's work that keeps me fit. Are you saying you won't love me anymore when I'm fat?"

Charlie cracked a smile, and her green eyes turned soft. "I doubt there will ever be a day where you're fat, but I'll still love you if that day ever comes."

Fuck, yeah, she would.

Grabbing the base of my dick, I squeezed as I moved closer to the tub. "This tub was a great idea. I have to thank whoever thought to put it in."

"I think I'm going to make it part of my daily routine." Her hands went to her breasts, where she started to massage and squeeze them together. With each movement of her hands, I got a flash of her pretty pink nipples.

I slowly stroked my cock, and as I watched, Charlie tilted her head back and moaned. "Sin." My name came out like a plea. I couldn't take it anymore. If I wasn't inside of her in the next minute, I was going to combust.

"Sit forward, Charlie," I demanded.

Her eyes popped open. Sliding forward, she hugged her knees to her chest to give me enough room to get in behind her, my legs bracketing her body. Charlie got up on her knees between my legs and turned to face me.

"Why is it so hot when a guy touches himself?" Her hand skirted down between her legs. I watched as her fingers disappeared inside her tight cunt. My dick was desperate to be where her fingers were.

"It's the same when I watch you touch yourself. I can't help but want to be deep inside of you while you use your fingers to bring yourself to completion."

Moving forward, Charlie straddled my legs and lined herself up with my waiting cock. Slowly lowering herself, she pressed her chest to mine. The hard peaks of her nipples brushed my chest as Charlie leaned forward and kissed along my jaw. "How about we make that a reality?"

Gripping her by the waist, I surged my hips forward and impaled her with my cock. The feel of her pussy contracting as she adjusted nearly had me losing my shit. Somehow, I managed to hold it together for a little while longer.

Charlie's smooth body glided against mine. My hands roamed every inch of skin I could touch. The feel of her hand moving between her legs and touching my dick as she rode me set my body on fire. My balls started to tingle, and I knew I wouldn't last much longer. Grabbing her by the hips, I moved Charlie up and down my cock faster and faster, even as water splashed out onto the floor. I didn't care if we made a mess. All I cared about was staking my claim on Charlie and making her mine. I wanted my cum to be permanently imprinted on her body, letting every person who crossed her path know Charlie belonged to me. The thought sent me over the edge.

"You're mine," I grunted as I shot off inside her. With each pulse of my cock, my ownership of her solidified.

Charlie's walls were still quaking around me when I finally came down. I held her to me and kissed up the column of her neck. Her body slumped against mine as she melted into me. She rested her head on my shoulder. I could feel the flutter of her eyelashes against my neck and the light pants of her breath.

"Do you want to get out?"

"No, I want to stay exactly like this for a little longer. Soon you'll be back to work, and I won't get to do this whenever I want."

Running my hands up and down her back, I leaned back and enjoyed the feel of Charlie, soft and relaxed against me. "If you want me to jump into a bath with you, morning, noon, or night, all you have to do is call me. I'll be here faster than you can fill this big ass tub up."

After several long minutes of silence, Charlie shifted her arm to wrap around my side. "I still don't know what to do about work. Randy isn't answering my calls, so I don't even know if there's a job to go back to."

"He'd be stupid not to have you back, but you can open up your own gallery if he doesn't. Or do whatever you want. We can set up a space here for you to paint. Seriously, the world is your oyster. Do what your heart is telling you to do. I'll support you on anything you want to do."

Sitting up, Charlie cupped my cheek and ran her thumb over the stubble, her green eyes trailing over my face. "You really mean that, don't you?"

I wasn't so good with words, but I could express to her how I felt with my body. Leaning forward, I kissed her, showing her how I would give her the world. All she had to do was ask. I'd once lost Charlie thinking it would be the best for both of us, but instead, we both suffered for years. Now the only thing that could separate us now was death.

We broke apart, panting. Charlie shivered in my arms now that the water had grown cold. I stood with her in my arms.

"Put me down." She tried to slide out of my grip, but I tightened my hold on her. "Sin," she tried to chastise me, but I wasn't having it. "You're still injured."

"Stop fighting me," I grumbled as I stepped out of the tub. "I'm fully capable of holding my woman." I felt her body go laze against me. When I looked down at her,

Charlie's face was so full of love I almost stumbled. I walked her over to the bed and sat her down before I went back and got the food I'd brought in. "I haven't had the chance to feed you yet, but first, I think you need to find your clothes. I'm not sure I'll be able to eat with those lush tits staring at me." Especially if I saw my cum dripping out of her.

"I agree," she licked her lips. Charlie cocked her head to the side and looked me up and down. "Do you think it will always be like this?"

"Like what?" I held out my hand and helped her off the bed.

Her small hand touched my back as we descended the stairs. "Ravenous for each other all the time."

When we reached the bottom floor, I pulled her in front of me and wrapped my arms around her waist. "I hope not. I want you more now than I ever did when we were in high school."

Her emerald eyes looked up at me, and all I wanted to do was sink into their depths. "I've been waiting for you every day since the day…" She swallowed harshly and looked to the side. "It's still so hard to think about. Even knowing that nothing happened. Promise me you won't sacrifice yourself again for my wellbeing."

I was already shaking my head before she finished talking. "I can't do that. I would take a bullet to spare your life or keep you from pain. The only thing I can promise you is I won't make a decision that will affect the rest of our lives without talking to you first unless it's life or death."

"I guess that's as good of a compromise as I'm going to get." She leaned forward with her hands on my chest. "And I'm going to make it impossible for you to ever let me go again."

"You've already done that, Charlie. I'm not going to put either of us through that misery again. I hadn't felt whole in ten long damn years, and I was put back together again with one look, one touch. It wrecked me all over again, knowing I'd only get to keep you for such a short amount of time."

"I'm yours, Sin." Her words were breathy as they hit my skin and sunk deep into my heart. "In every way that counts."

"And I'm yours. Until the end of time and then some." I pulled her flush against me, needing to claim her at least once before moving from our spot. Eventually, we'd come up for air and food. Until then, I would mark every inch of her inside and out to let the world know Charlotte Hunter was mine.

Did you enjoy SIN'S SACRIFICE If so, please consider leaving a review on Goodreads, Amazon, or BookBub. Reviews mean the world to authors especially to authors who are starting out. You can help get your favorite books into the hands of new readers.

I'd appreciate your help in spreading the word and it will only take a moment to leave a quick review. It can be as short or as long as you like. Your review could be the deciding factor or whether or not someone else buys my book.

To stay up to date on all my releases subscribe to my newsletter. https://ellakade.com/newsletter/

ACKNOWLEDGMENTS

My family- your support means so much. Thank you for all of your encouragement and giving me the time to do what makes me happy.

Misty Walker: Thank you for giving the confidence to write West and Fin's story and always answering all my outrageous questions.

Wendy: You're my champion. Thank you for pushing me when I need it, and for rooting for and every character I write.

Kelsey: If it wasn't for our online writing, I'm not sure how many books I'd get done. Thank you for always being there.

To my **girls**: QB Tyler , Carmel Rhodes, Erica Marselas. I love each and every one of you. Thank you for all of your support.

Thank you **Kristen Breanne** for making my story into a book.

To all my **author friends**, you know who you are. Thank you for accepting me and making me feel welcome in this amazing community.

To **Wildfire Marketing Solutions and Shauna**, thank you for all your knowledge and for helping me make Away Game a success!

Lovers thank you for always being there.

Team Harlow's Girls: Each and everyone of you are amazing. Thank you for all of your support. You ROCK!

To each and every **reader**, **reviewer**, and **blogger** - I would be nowhere without you. Thank you for taking a chance on an unknown author.

ABOUT ELLA

Ella Kade is a forbidden and dark romance writer who enjoys writing captivating characters with sinful intent.

Read Ella to get immersed into her words where she ruins lives and slowly puts them back together.

ALSO BY ELLA KADE

<u>Willow Bay Series - Forbidden Romance</u>

Away Game - MM, Bully

First Down - Sister's Best Friend

Over Time - MM, Student/Teacher

Off Sides - Second Chance, Forbidden - September 26, 2022

The Elite's: Year Two- Secret Society

Sin's Sacrifice - MC, Second Chance

King's Vow - Secret Society, Drug Cartel, Bodyguard, Reverse
Age Gap - December 12, 2022